Double the Dream

Lois Carroll

Double the Dream

by Lois Carroll

Cover Artist: Nancy Donahue
Editor: Tricia Isham
Printed in the United States of America

Published by
WHISKEY CREEK PRESS LLC
Whiskeycreekpress.com

Print ISBN: 978-1-61160-826-7

Dedication

For my readers who keep my dream alive.

Chapter 1

"I can't remember what they look like. How can we find two men I wouldn't recognize?"

Anna Anderssen sighed at her younger sister Katrin's complaint. It wasn't the first time she'd heard it. "They lived on a farm not far away and came into town once a week back in Norway. We saw them once in a while."

"But they left to find jobs on other farms, because their family farm couldn't support all the sons. That was three or four years ago when I was a child. I haven't seen them since then."

"I know, but I remember what they look like. Don't worry. All we need are their names to ask if someone knows them. We'll find them," Anna assured her.

"I don't know," Katrin countered. "I was barely grown when Ingor left for America."

"Well, you're seventeen now and I'm over a year older. You remember Lars, don't you? He just left for America a year ago. The letter he sent his uncle said that he had made it to Philadelphia and was leaving to look for his brother in Dakota Territory. They're both settled there by now."

"If he found his brother."

"The Dakota Territory can't be so big that he would disappear. We're old enough to manage on our own and find them."

Katrin looked up at her and frowned.

"Believe me. We'll find them," Anna stated firmly. Smiling to make her sister feel more confident, she added, "We can't marry them if we can't find them."

Katrin drew in a quick breath. “Oh, no, what will we do if we can’t find them?” Katrin asked, her eyes wide with fright. “We’ll be all alone and have no way to support ourselves.”

Anna groaned and realized she’s said the wrong thing. “Katrin, please. Don’t worry. We’ve reached New York and now let’s keep up with the other passengers in this line so we can leave this ship.” They shuffled forward a few steps and set their larger bag down but held on to the strap.

Standing at the rail of the ship, they looked over the line of immigrants. They all had been waiting to be allowed to leave the ship. The line moved very slowly as had the weeks they’d spent on board crossing the ocean from Norway.

Their destination, Castle Garden, had sounded like such a beautiful place—the perfect spot to disembark the ship and begin their journey west across the United States. Thinking about the lovely place made the weeks of seasickness worth it. But when they arrived at the mooring at the pier in New York City, Anna and Katrin saw no flowers, no greenery, and certainly no castle. They wondered at first if they had docked in the wrong place.

When they arrived, the passengers swarmed toward the gangplank only to be stopped by the crew before being able to leave the ship. They were told to line up according to the number on the piece of paper given to each of them the day before they docked. The resulting line curled around the deck and seemed endless.

“That is the order you must follow to leave the ship and go through the immigration process,” the man next to the gangplank shouted. “And don’t lose the number or you go to the end of the line,” he warned. “We’ll take as many as possible today and the rest tomorrow.”

Anna and Katrin looked at their high numbers on the papers that probably meant another night onboard the ship. Others with even higher numbers had tried to trade with them, but they would have none of it.

They were most anxious to get off the ship and get on with their journey to find their husbands-to-be.

"At least the ship is not rolling in port," Katrin said as they tried to get to sleep their last night on board. "My stomach is not so upset."

"I almost feel hungry again," Anna said with a little laugh.

When their turn finally came to disembark, they followed in line along the pier. From there the line snaked across an unkempt yard toward a well-worn building. Several panes of glass in the windows were cracked or broken out, and the paint was peeling.

Once inside, other immigrants with large trunks and heavy suitcases were ordered to leave them in an area to the side. Anna could make out some of the murmurs from people worried that they might not ever see their cases again.

"I'm glad we decided not to bring a trunk," Anna said. Katrin nodded.

The sisters trudged on, each clutching two cloth hand-sewn bags. Their small bag containing two more dresses plus two skirts and two blouses for each of them along with their nightgowns, their small clothes, and several pairs of stockings. Tucked in the corners were the personal necessities like a hairbrush, sewing needles and thread, a long apron, a few ribbons to contain their long blonde hair, and a protective cloth bonnet they brought to wear in the sun. These bags held all the money they had too. It was in a small drawstring sack that was tucked under their clothes for safekeeping. That was the main reason the sisters never let these sacks get out of their sight.

The bottom of these bags took on a square shape from the books they carried in them. They each had a copy of the smallest Bible they could find. They were printed in Norwegian, as were the three other books that Katrin had chosen. Anna had selected a book of short stories that was printed in English in addition to two others in her native tongue. She thought the book of stories would help them to practice their English by reading to each other. In any case they knew they would have long hours to pass on their journey and the books would be handy.

Their other larger bag, also made of sturdy cloth and double sewn at the seams, contained the quilts the women of their village had gifted them plus the fancy dresses that would be their wedding dresses when they found the Oleson brothers. They would have to do for special occasions after the weddings, too. There were a few lengths of fabric that could be made into clothes later for them or for babies. These bags also held the few items they had made and brought to America for their married life. They were small things like embroidered napkins and pieces of handmade lace for a collar or cuffs. They didn't add much weight and it made the sisters feel good about having something special with them. They carried these larger bags hung from their shoulders on wide cloth straps that they had fashioned to make carrying them easier.

The only items deemed frivolous by their mother, who helped them pack, were the pairs of shoes of more delicate leather that each carried in the larger bags. Standing in the line waiting to board the ship in port in Norway, it hadn't taken them long to put two of the books and the Bible in their shoulder bag. They could exchange them when they wanted new reading material and in the meantime, the handbag they carried close to their chests to keep their money safe was less heavy.

"I wish the Oleson brothers had written more often to tell us where to find them," Katrin complained.

"Yes. Ingor wrote only once after arriving in Dakota Territory. I remember he described how much of the way to Dakota Territory he had to walk so his horse was not overworked."

"I hope we don't have to walk," Katrin said. "These shoes are very stiff and uncomfortable."

"They are new. They will soften with time."

"I hope you're right."

"Remember how Ingor told of clothes and even furniture that folks traveling west had left along the road that was too much weight for their stock to keep pulling in their wagon?" Anna asked.

"I wish we knew exactly how we will be traveling west," Katrin said, stepping forward a meter as the line moved on.

"We'll find the way, and we've already pared down what we would take so we won't have to leave any of it on the trail."

Katrin knelt on one knee and then the other and loosened the laces on her shoes. "That's better," she said upon standing again. "We don't look at all fashionable in these shoes."

"Just keep them hidden under your skirts as much as possible."

Their wool coats, with hand knit scarves and mittens stuffed into the big pockets, hung over their arms. Waiting in line in the sun, they felt the spring morning was warm enough not to need to wear them. Their dress hats with a flat brim that they wore squarely on the top of their heads shaded their faces somewhat.

"The longer we stand in the sun, the more I wish we had worn our bonnets that would shade our whole faces and necks, too," Anna remarked.

Katrin shook her head. "I'm glad we chose these hats that are more the fashion. I think they make us blend in with others."

Anna looked around. "I don't think we need worry about our hats being in fashion here," she said.

"People are dressed as they would be at home, wherever that was," Katrin put in.

"We all have more to think about than our clothes or hats," Anna said with a grin. "Besides, we shouldn't worry about attracting men with our clothes now. We are on our way to be married."

The line moved forward several steps. The sisters picked up their larger bags and moved with others toward the building. Before long they were at the head of the line.

"He's waving toward us," Katrin said, tugging on Anna's sleeve and pointing toward the open doorway.

"Keep moving this way," the man shouted.

Following his direction, they entered a large room in the center of the building. The sisters looked around, trying to figure out where they were to go next. So many different languages were being spoken that it was unsettling. Though both sisters spoke English, they had difficulty picking it out among all the other languages they heard.

Parents were shouting to keep their children in line. Babies were crying. The men directing everyone were shouting to be heard, and they all used arm movements that cut across language barriers to direct people into the proper lines.

"In that line first," a man shouted, looking right at them, his arm pointing toward a line entering another room.

"These must be the doctors," Katrin whispered as they followed the line and finally could see into the room. The sisters stood straighter and waited while a man in a stained white coat listened to their chests while they breathed deeply before he looked into their mouths.

"You're healthy," he said to each of them despite their still feeling somewhat weak from having been seasick for weeks on shipboard.

A broad smile appeared on their faces for the first time since stepping onto American soil. They had been pronounced healthy and would not be prevented from traveling on to the Dakota Territory to find their husbands-to-be. While they did still have to figure out how to make the trip, they hugged each other and laughed with relief.

The man beside the doctor directed them toward long tables in the center of the main room. Signs on the table identified the languages spoken by the men working there. Relieved to find an official there who spoke Norwegian so they could be certain they understood the whole process, they listened as the remainder of the immigration procedure was finally explained.

Next they were able to exchange the money they had brought from home for American dollars. The number of dollars that they received seemed small though, and they began to worry about being able to afford the cost of travel left before them.

"What if we run out of money?" Katrin whispered. "What will we do?"

"We just won't run out," Anna replied firmly but just as softly. She smiled. "We can be very careful about what we spend."

"And don't believe anyone who tells you that Confederate dollars are worth more," the man warned them as they split the American money between them and hid it again in their handmade purses. "They're not worth a thing, so you don't want to trade money with anyone."

"These dollars are good in the Dakota Territory?" Anna asked.

"The only thing better would be gold," he replied with a laugh. "Not many places to spend it out there though. That where you ladies are headed?"

"Yes, sir. We find the Oleson brothers. They will be our husbands," Katrin announced.

Anna had not thought that her explanation of their goal was at all funny, but the man laughed heartily. The sisters stepped back a bit and watched him with wide eyes. "What is funny about that?" Katrin whispered to Anna.

When the man saw their startled reaction to his laughter, he stopped. "Sorry, but it's a big empty territory out there. Good luck finding your men." He put an X on the small paper beside the numbers they had been given on shipboard to identify themselves and called out, "Next."

"But where is the train to Chicago? Where do we go next?" the sisters chorused in panicked voices before they could be ushered away.

The man rose off his stool and pointed toward a large open doorway at the end of the building. "Go right out through there. You get on the wagons sitting there and don't go beyond them. There's too many people in the city out there who would like to steal your money and…and well, you don't need to know the rest of what they are after."

"The wagon takes us to the train?"

"Yes, and you can buy food for your trip at those tables over there where it's safe. Once you're crossing the city, you don't want to take your money out of them bags. Don't let anyone even know you have any or where you keep it."

"But the tickets for the train to Chicago?"

"Oh, right." He thought a moment and gave them an amount that he thought would cover two tickets. "Put that where you can get to it easy and hide the rest."

"Thank you, thank you," Anna and Katrin chorused.

He just went right on to the next immigrant in line and paid no more attention to the sisters who went on to the food sale table. With bread and cheese plus some apples in each of their bags and the money for the train tickets hidden deep in Anna's skirt pocket, they hid the remainder of their cash again in their small bags. Finished at Castle Garden, the sisters walked out the large door into the sunlight.

"Your wagon takes us to the train station where we can get a train to Chicago?" Anna asked the man beside the lead wagon to double-check what they had been told. The sisters couldn't afford to make any mistakes now.

"That's where we're headed, ma'am. Let me help you up."

He gave the sisters a hand so they could climb up into the wagon and sit on the wooded plank seats built around the outside. The center of the wagon was filling with the bags and cases belonging to the other passengers already sitting in the wagon.

The woman seated next to Anna said something to her, but it was in a language that Anna had never heard.

"I'm sorry, but I don't understand what you are saying," she replied in Norwegian.

She was about to ask her in English if she spoke that language, but a couple who was just climbing up into the wagon had heard what she said and replied in the same language. The two couples never stopped speaking to each other after that.

"I wonder what they are talking about," Katrin said softly.

"Perhaps they've found out they are headed for the same place," Anna replied.

"I wish we could be that lucky."

Anxious to get to the train station, they didn't like having to wait, because the wagons to the trains stood still until full. When the horses did finally move the wagons along the crowded streets, the sisters were amazed.

"I have never seen so many people in one place as in this city of New York," Katrin remarked.

"Street after street the buildings are built so close together that there are no lawns or open spaces between them. And they are so tall. Look, they are taller than the mayor's house back home."

"Hey, out of the way," the driver suddenly shouted at children playing right in the streets where wagons and carriages vied for the right of way.

The sisters turned in their seats to watch the children as they passed.

"Everything is so different from our Norwegian village where there are flowers and green grass around the homes and plenty of safe places for the children to play." Katrin shook her head. "I would not like living in this city. I hope the Dakota Territory is not like this."

"I don't think it can be, because they are just now trying to get more people to move there."

They turned a corner and both sisters as well as the rest of the passengers covered their noses and mouths with their sleeves to avoid the stench coming from a pile of garbage on the side of the street.

"I'm glad the Dakota Territory isn't like this," Anna said when they had passed it.

"Here's your stop for the trains," the driver shouted as he tied the reins to the brake handle that he had set. "Everybody gets out here." He jumped down from his perch and walked to the back of the wagon to give a hand to the passengers climbing down and then to pull the trunks to the edge where they could reach them.

Startled by the rush of everyone getting off the wagon, the sisters sat clutching their bags until they could get off safely. They followed the others, but hadn't walked far toward the trains when they suddenly found themselves in a sea of blue. Not the blue water of the huge ocean they had crossed from their homes to land in New York, but a sea of dark blue uniforms, some rather ragged and dirty and others cleaner. Both seas of blue were just as terrifying.

Never having seen so many soldiers in one place, the sisters looped arms to keep together in the jostling crowd and clutched their bags and coats to their chests with trembling hands. They had to force their trembling legs to move them toward the huge black engines. Black smoke belched from their tall smoke stacks and steam shot out sporadically between the huge metal wheels.

Tall enough to see the trains over some of the other people around them, Anna suddenly stopped. "I don't know which one is the train we need to take," she admitted, speaking in Norwegian. "None of the signs say they are going west. Some have names, but I do not know them. Can you see one that says Chicago?"

"No. There must be someone we can ask," Katrin said.

"Watch it there, soldier. Give those ladies an inch to breathe in," a big man in blue, carrying a gun as long as his leg, yelled as soldiers marched past close by them.

The sisters stopped and tried to move out of their way. "What are they doing?" Katrin asked in a small voice.

"I don't know. Just stay close until they pass," Anna told her.

All the conversations around them were more like tenor and bass rumbles than real words. No one else was speaking Norwegian, but unlike in Castle Garden, they did recognize most of the words and phrases as being English. Getting worried, the sisters didn't know where to go while everyone else was rushing about them as if their train were about to depart.

"What if the train leaves without us because we don't know which one it is?" Katrin asked, clutching her sister's arm.

In Norway they had been so happy, so excited at the prospect of coming to America to find Ole's nephews, but they didn't feel that way now. America was a scary place and they didn't know which way to turn or how to get help.

"I wish we had never come," Katrin whispered.

"Please don't start that again," Anna insisted, trying to stand a little straighter so she could see more. "We agreed to do this when Mr. Oleson selected us to come here to marry his nephews. If we stay together it can't be too much for us to figure out."

"Then tell me which one is our train," Katrin pleaded.

"I don't know, but we'll find it," Anna said to calm her sister.

"We can't delay. We have to get to Dakota Territory before winter sets in."

"But its only spring now. It's the month of May, Katrin. I don't know how fast the trains move, but we will be fine."

"Yes, but Ingor's letter said it took him months."

"But he didn't ride the train. That can't take months, can it?" Anna asked.

"No, I guess not."

Though distracted from their efforts by the soldiers surrounding them, Anna held her sister's arm firmly. She would not let them get separated. But looking at the soldiers, she realized they had paused when the sisters did and stood around them instead of passing them by. With broad grins on their faces as they whipped off their uniform hats, they looked the sisters over from head to toe.

The sisters stood where they were, but it wasn't easy. The close observation made their hearts beat more rapidly. Their heads pounded as heat rose up their necks and into their cheeks.

"Be strong," Anna urged as they pressed against each other instead of running away.

"They gonna be on our train, Sarge?" one soldier asked without looking away from the sisters. "They goin' to Chicago?"

Anna looked at the soldier directly. Was it possible she had heard Chicago? "Train to Chicago," she asked, her voice cracking. "Which is train to Chicago?" she said more firmly after clearing her throat. She prayed that she had heard his word correctly. "He did say Chicago, didn't he?" she asked her sister in Norwegian.

"Hey, is she going to Chicago?" the young man beside them said, reluctantly turning from looking at the ladies to the sergeant.

"Pardon me, but are you ladies looking for the train to Chicago?" a voice from behind them said in perfect Norwegian before the tall sergeant had a chance to speak.

Tears of relief burning their eyes, they released the nervous breaths they had each been holding and spun around toward the most-welcome sound of their own language. A tall soldier with a broad smile on his face stood directly behind them.

"Oh, yes, sir," Anna replied in Norwegian, a smile on her face. "Can you tell us which train will take us to Chicago?"

"I'll do better than that. I'll take you to it, but allow me to introduce myself. I am Adam Johnson, in charge of this motley troupe that so rudely surrounds you," he continued in Norwegian. "I hope they haven't bothered you."

"Thank you, sir. No, sir." Anna, not really sure if she should or not, introduced herself and her younger sister Katrin. "We are most thankful that you speak in words we can understand very easily," Anna added. "We speak English, but we worry we will miss some important words."

"I understand," he replied easily. "Do you have your tickets?"

"No, sir, we need tickets to Chicago. From there we must find our way to the Dakota Territory."

The lieutenant suddenly smiled broadly but didn't explain why. "That's a long way beyond where the trains go. But first things first," he announced. "The ticket booth is over there." He extended his arm, pointing to the right of the trains. "I was on my way there, and you are welcome to come with me."

He ordered the sergeant to assemble the men and their families together and to stay there. "I will return with our passes as soon as I can."

Deciding they could trust a kind soldier, Anna and Katrin followed him. As they wove through the crowd toward the ticket window, they agreed in whispers that Lieutenant Johnson was a godsend. Once there he helped them purchase the correct tickets and get the correct change before he turned in the paper that arranged for his men and their families to ride the same train.

"They've been waiting for you, Lieutenant. They'll be glad to see you've arrived."

His transaction complete, the lieutenant led the ladies to the proper track where they could board their train with his men and the women and children traveling with them.

Despite the loads they already carried along with their rifles, the soldiers offered to carry the sisters' bags. "You are kind to offer, but we can manage," Anna said in English as they held on to them tightly. They didn't want the bags out of their hands, because they contained all they owned. To lose one was unthinkable. Then they would have nothing.

As they walked down the platform, they passed men and women pushing small carts with a variety of food and drink. Because of the warnings the sisters had heard in Castle Garden about not buying food in the city, they only purchased two bottles of milk with a little of the change from the tickets when they saw many of the soldiers doing the same. They had not had anything to drink since a small meal on shipboard that morning, and they didn't see any place to get a drink of water.

"It's a long ride," the lieutenant said as he bought several items for his supper. "You don't want to get any food now? I don't know if they'll have any on the train."

"We have enough for a day or two in our bags," Anna assured him. She hoped they would not be on the train any longer than that.

Holding the bottles rather than packing them, lest they leak, the sisters followed as the lieutenant led them to a conductor, who checked their tickets. The first to be allowed to enter the car, the lieutenant directed the sisters to a seat in the back of the car opposite the one he would occupy.

"If you sit here fewer people will bother you passing down the aisle. Here, I'll put your bags on the rack over your head," the lieutenant offered. The larger ones stowed, he reached for the smaller ones.

"Oh, no," Anna insisted. "We will keep these here in the seat with us. All our food is in these bags." She didn't add that the bags held all their money, too, and they would not let them out of their sight.

"Fine, and I'm thinking you'll want to keep your coats to roll as pillows or to keep you warm enough to sleep in these seats tonight."

"Then we won't be sorry that we had to carry them."

"They'll come in handy in Dakota Territory, too. It still gets mighty cold up there. But that's a long way off yet."

The sisters frowned and looked at each other. They wondered how long would it take to travel to "a long way off".

As they talked, soldiers filed past them and sat in the seats closest to them. A number of the men who had women and children with them sat in the seats closer to the front of the car. While Anna and Katrin settled into their seat, the lieutenant left the car and returned helping an elderly woman and a small boy of about 5 or so to a seat several rows in front of them.

After staying to talk with them a while, he returned to his own seat opposite the sisters. He stowed his bag and rifle in its scabbard on the overhead rack. He picked up his hat that he had left in the middle of the seats meant to hold two people to mark them as taken and put it back on his head before he sat down.

Anna looked over at the lieutenant and found him looking at her. Taking the opportunity to talk to him, she asked what she and her sister had been talking about but hadn't figured out. "Lieutenant, can you tell me why your soldiers are traveling with their families? We have not seen soldiers in Norway do this."

"No, I don't suppose so. Our platoon has been reassigned to Fort Abercrombie and the men who have families can move them out there, too. They will live near the fort."

"You have a great many people to keep track of. I think they are fortunate to have you to lead them," Anna said, and then she blushed, realizing how personal her compliment had been.

"We certainly appreciate the help you have given us," Katrin put in.

"Well, you ladies will be perfectly safe here. Just let me know if you need anything more," the lieutenant offered before he leaned forward and tapped the arm of the soldier in the seat in front of the sisters. "Sergeant."

The man he addressed jumped to his feet to stand at attention, but hit his head on the overhead rack. He grunted and rubbed his head, and then quickly moved into the aisle and raised his hand to salute the lieutenant.

"At ease, Sergeant. No more bounding up while we're on the train. All the men can remain at ease."

"Yes, sir. Thank you, sir."

"These women are headed for the Dakota Territory so they will be traveling with us. I hope you'll keep an eye out for them as well as the others."

"Oh, yes sir. Thank you, sir."

The sergeant glanced over at the sisters and touched his hand to the rim of his hat in a salute. "Ma'am," he said, looking at Anna and then Katrin. Instead of looking away, his gaze rested on Katrin. Blushing prettily, Katrin smiled at him.

"Thank you, Sergeant," she said. Then, realizing that Anna was frowning at her, she looked down at her hands that were folded on her lap.

"Sergeant, take a count of the men, will you? I don't want to leave anyone here. They should all be in this car and the one behind us. They must have the horses about loaded by now so we should be ready to leave soon."

"Yes, sir," he replied, finally looking away from Katrin to the lieutenant.

The sergeant walked to the far end of the car and then passed down the aisle counting the soldiers. He went on into the car behind them and returned minutes later to report the count to the lieutenant.

Before he sat down, the sergeant smiled again at Anna and Katrin. "It's a pleasure to have you traveling with us, ladies," he said in English with a Scottish accent that was not unusual for them to hear back in Norway. "I'm Sergeant Tavis McDougal. You let me know if you need help with anything. I'll be happy to oblige."

"Thank you, Sergeant," Anna said.

"Yes, thank you." Katrin got in with a warm smile.

The Sergeant smiled back at her. "I hail from Glasgow, and I know what it's like to come across the sea and then be thrown into a sea of strangers here. It's quite different from back home, I'm sure."

"Yes, and it's very kind of you to offer to help should we need it," Katrin added boldly with an eagerness that made Anna look in her direction to be certain she had interpreted it correctly in her voice. From the broad smile on Katrin's face, Anna was convinced that she had heard it.

The sergeant smiled a few moments longer, looking at Katrin, and then sat down. The soldier sitting beside him turned back and smiled, too, but after getting a jab from the sergeant's elbow, he said nothing and turned back forward.

Chapter 2

A blend of delicious smells soon filled the railroad car as the passengers ate the food they had bought on the platform or carried with them. Parched and tired after their trek across city streets in the wooden wagon, Anna and Katrin shared one of their bottles of milk. It quickly disappeared with some of their bread and cheese as well. The food went a long way to making their stomachs feel normal again and not upset as they had been on shipboard.

While they ate, the lieutenant had walked forward again, apparently to check on the boy and the elderly woman he had helped before. He seemed to be such a caring man, Anna thought. It was a surprise to her to find his caring quality in an officer in the Army. She thought all the soldiers would be hardened to the plights of the people around them.

The sisters took out books to read to pass the time as they waited for the train to leave the station. "Look," Katrin whispered to Anna sometime later. "The lieutenant is coming back. You can ask him now where the necessary is."

"How can I ask a man that?" She could feel the heat in her cheeks at the thought of asking a man such a question.

"Because we need to find one."

Anna shook her head. "I couldn't do that."

"Well, no one has moved from their seats, and I can't believe they all don't need one, too!"

"We can wait a little longer."

"Or maybe one of us should go ask one of the women sitting with the families," Katrin proposed.

The sisters looked at the women sitting ahead of them and then over at the lieutenant and smiled. He tipped his hat at them. "Have you ladies been on a train like this before?"

"Oh, no," Anna replied. "There is no train where we lived."

"We drove in a small wagon with one horse when we needed to go somewhere, but we never had so many miles to cross as there are here," Katrin added.

He nodded. "Then...ah, let me explain the train a little. If you get tired of sitting, you are welcome to stand up and walk in the aisle for a while. The ride is not smooth so you may need to hold the back of the aisle seat as you walk." He looked forward down the aisle. "You'll see the...the necessary is at the far end of this car. It's that door on the side at the end," he explained with a gesture of his arm to point out which side. "You just have to take your turn along with all the rest of us once the train is moving out of the city."

"We must wait until the train is moving?" Katrin asked, concern in her voice.

"Yes. They keep the door locked until then."

"Thank you." Anna glanced at Katrin with a look meant to silence her. She was thankful for the information they had needed to know, but she felt the heat rising up in her cheeks all over again.

"It will be handy to have it so close," Katrin continued soft enough for just Anna to hear.

"That's enough about it," Anna urged just as softly. She leaned back in her seat and turned to look out the window.

Anna hoped that this necessary would be nicer than the chamber pots on shipboard. In the room where they slept with many other women, there had been only four with little privacy at any of them. And they were never emptied often enough.

However, later, when Anna entered the one on the train, she found it very disconcerting to look down the wide tube and see the wooden railroad ties racing past. No wonder they could not use it when they were in a station. The tube emptied right onto the ties. That would be most unpleasant to have happen in a station.

When the train finally started moving, she could see the little boy, who had been friendly with the lieutenant, standing in his seat and pointing out the window beside the elderly woman. Then he jumped off the seat and raced up the aisle toward the lieutenant. He saw the boy coming and put out an arm that caught him and lifted him into his lap. The boy laughed with delight.

"We're moving! The train is moving," the boy said. Grinning broadly, he added, "And we're moving so fast." He pointed out the window beyond the lieutenant. "See?"

Anna realized that she easily understood what the boy was saying, because he was speaking Norwegian, too. The lieutenant laughed and moved over toward the window to make room for the boy to sit beside him.

"But I can't see out the window from here," the boy complained.

The lieutenant lifted him onto his lap so he was facing the window. "That better?"

"Yes." The boy's attention was clearly on the sights passing outside the window. He and the lieutenant discussed the houses, and then the river they rode along where they saw some fishermen sitting beside the water.

"Will we be able to fish when we get to our new home?"

"I hope so. The Army should give me time off to teach you how to fish in the Red River that flows not far from the fort."

The boy grinned, but his gaze was back out the window. "Look! There are only a few houses by the river now. Oh, there's a boat. I hope Grandmother can see this, too."

"Maybe you should go back and tell her what you saw." The lieutenant lifted the boy from his lap and set him in the aisle pointed toward the seat up forward where his grandmother was looking back at them. "Your grandmother looks worried. Does she have a reason?"

"Oh," the boy said, dropping his head. "I should have told her where I was going."

"Yes. So next time you remember to tell her what you are doing before you run to see me. Then when you leave her side, she will know where you will be. We don't want her to have to worry about where you are."

"Yes, sir."

The lieutenant looked at Anna who had been watching the boy. "But, before you go back to your seat," he said to the boy while keeping eye contact with Anna, "I want to introduce you to Miss Anna Anderssen and her sister Miss Katrin. They are from Norway, too."

A smile reappeared on the boy's face. "I'm happy to meet you," he said politely.

"And we're pleased to meet you," Anna replied for both of them. "But I didn't get your name."

"I'm Eric Johnson, and when I'm old enough, I'm going to be a soldier, too." Done with the niceties, the boy turned back to the lieutenant. "Just like you. Aren't I, Father?"

The lieutenant smiled and ruffled the boy's hair. "Yes, son, but right now you had better go back to your grandmother. She'll be lonely without you to keep her company."

The boy ran back up the aisle to his seat. Anna glanced at the lieutenant to find him looking at her. "He is a very good little boy."

"I hope he didn't bother you. This is his first train ride. Everything is new to him."

"It is good that you and your men can take families with you," Anna said.

He nodded. "There are homes nearby the fort where they will live and only go into the fort if there's trouble with the Indians."

Anna wanted to ask about the trouble with the Indians, but at the same time, she didn't want to worry Katrin. She glanced at her sister whose attention was divided between the conversation and the view out the window beside her seat.

Looking back across the aisle, Anna asked, "And your wife? Isn't she going?"

The smile was immediately erased from the lieutenant's face. He shook his head. "She died giving birth to Eric. Her mother, our only living relative, took over caring for Eric. She speaks mostly Norwegian, but Eric has learned English from other children where they lived in New York."

"I'm sorry she is gone," Anna said softly. "Raising a son while in the Army must be difficult."

He looked at her and nodded, continuing the private talk in soft tones. "I haven't been able to see him much with the Army moving me around. I don't know what I'd do without his grandmother to help. She came from Norway to be here when he was born and stayed to live with him while I was fighting. I will always be grateful for her help."

Anna smiled. "But now you will all be together in Dakota Territory."

He nodded and she relaxed back in her seat. She glanced at her silent sister and realized that Katrin had fallen asleep beside her, her head leaning against the window. The exhausting day had caught up with them both. Anna stifled a yawn and glanced at the lieutenant to see if he had noticed. He had and she laughed a bit with her embarrassment.

He smiled and removed his hat. "I think your sister has the right idea. We should take the opportunity to nap when we can get it. Sleeping sitting up isn't easy." He pulled his hat down over his eyes as he leaned back against his window, sitting at an angle in his double seat.

As she made herself more comfortable in her seat, Anna knew she wouldn't have any trouble falling asleep. She glanced back at the lieutenant but could no longer see his face. She couldn't help but wonder if the Oleson brothers were as handsome as he was. The letter Ingor had written from Dakota Territory said he had grown a beard to protect his face from the cold wind and snow. She wasn't sure she would like a full beard covering a man's face. As soon as such thoughts entered her mind, she quickly tried to dismiss them. It wouldn't matter what they looked like. They were good, hard-working Norwegian men and would make wonderful husbands for her and her sister.

Feeling safe now instead of frightened with the Army surrounding them, she watched the countryside race by as they headed north to Albany on the first segment of their ride. The rocking of the car and the rhythmic clacking of the wheels on the tracks soon put her to sleep, too. She and her sister didn't sleep all through the night, but the sleep they managed to get along with the excitement of beginning their land voyage left them stronger and more optimistic about their travels.

The next morning, when the sky was barely gray instead of black, the lieutenant explained that several railroad companies owned sections of the route to Chicago. "We will have to change trains twice before we get there."

"Moving all the trunks and cases we saw on the platform will not be easy."

"And we have horses in the box cars to look out for, too. The railroad companies are laying down track as fast as they can, and some of the smaller ones are merging into a larger one," he added. "Before you know it, you'll be able to go all the way west on a train. That'll be something."

"I hope you will have the time to tell us how to find the coaches going west when we get to Chicago," Anna put in. "I don't want to be a bother, but we have no idea where to go."

"Don't worry about a thing. You just stay close to my men and their families. I'll be happy to help you however I can."

"That's very kind of you."

The smile on the lieutenant 's face went a long way to keeping Anna and her sister calm and confident. He held Anna's interest longer than she should let him, but she couldn't help but like him. His blond hair fell nearly to his shoulders, as did the hair of most of the soldiers. They all wore their uniform hats most of the time, but she soon realized that was probably because they had no place to store them safely. Their packs and long barreled weapons took up all the storage places over the seats. They even stretched over the sisters' larger bags where they lay on the rack above Katrin's head.

Once they reached Albany, the next train was easy to find, as the station was much smaller than in New York City. After the wait to transfer the trunks and the horses, they were headed in a westerly direction. They never passed through another city as large as New York City so most of their views were of the countryside. Being spring, many farmers were plowing their fields and planting their crops.

"These train rides don't seem to end. Isn't New York close to Chicago?" Katrin asked on the next day of travel after yet another switch to a new train.

"Now that we're on this train, we have just to ride through Ohio, along the border to Michigan, and then we'll come to the great lake of the same name. Before long after that we'll be entering the city of Chicago," the lieutenant explained. "It's a large city so you can tell easily when we get there."

"This is such a big country. Does it take days of travel to get everywhere, Lieutenant Johnson?" Anna asked.

He grinned and said, "Yes, but please, when we are talking together, I'd be happy to have you call me Adam. You probably wouldn't under different circumstances, but we will be traveling together for some time yet. It will be much easier."

The sisters looked at each other and silently agreed with a smile. "Thank you," Anna murmured. "And you must use our given names, too."

"Thank you. Anna is a very pretty name."

Anna smiled but looked away from his intense gaze.

"But your question was about the days it takes to travel to places here. This part of our journey on the trains can be measured in days, but once we leave Chicago, we have to travel in wagons or coaches. That is much slower. That part of the trip will take weeks."

"A letter that Ingor Oleson sent his uncle said it took him months to reach the Dakota Territory from the city called Philadelphia, but he didn't take the train. He rode his horse or walked the whole way," Anna explained.

"Travel is not easy on a horse or in a wagon, but it's the only way to travel when we go beyond the end of the tracks."

"Then you and your men are going beyond Chicago to your fort?"

"Yes, ma'am. Fort Abercrombie is on the Red River, in the eastern district of the Dakota Territory."

"You are going to the Dakota Territory, too?" Anna laughed and could not believe hearing such good news. Her heart beat more quickly and she clapped her hands together. "Did you hear that, Katrin?" Her sister nodded, a broad smile on her face, too. "I did not know. Oh, Adam, that is such good news. We can follow you and find our way." Realizing she had actually used his given name, she covered her mouth with the tips of her fingers. "Now I used your name already."

He smiled. "That's good. I think in a new country we all learn to do things differently from back home in the old country. And this is our home now."

"So many things are different than in our small village."

"More things than you can imagine."

He grinned and they went on to talk about all the different customs he'd seen during the fighting. He even mentioned people he'd seen who handle snakes as part of their religious service that he had seen in the South.

Anna thought the lieutenant was correct. Many customs were different here in America. Maybe she and Katrin should worry less about feeling different.

Speaking a common native language made her feel as if she and her sister had found a friend in Lieutenant Adam Johnson. She felt much better about their chances of finding the Oleson brothers. And when they found them, she was certain their husbands-to-be would have houses built already and furnished with all they could want. Their farm fields would be overflowing with crops. She just knew that life for them in their new home was going to be good.

* * * *

The next stop to change trains took longer than the switch in Albany, which was an unpleasant surprise because the station was the smallest one yet. Moving the horses and trunks gave the soldiers trouble at every turn. Eric had wanted to go with his father to see the horses being transferred, but Adam insisted that he stay with his grandmother.

"I want to know that you're safe. You can see the horses when we get to our destination," he told his son.

Eric grumbled as his father walked away, but he turned to help his grandmother with the bag of food that she carried. Anna and Katrin walked along side them. Moving slowly with all the others toward the next train, they were behind a family with a boy a year or two older than Eric. The boys had played together some on the train where they sat only a couple rows apart.

"You gotta stay with your grandmother," Jimmy taunted in a singsong manner that made Eric angry.

"You stop saying that," Eric shouted at him.

Rose, Jimmy's mother, took hold of him by his ear and pulled him a distance from Eric. "Jimmy-Bob, you start behaving right now or I'll call your Papa to come over and teach you how to behave. That boy's father is your pa's commander, and you will be nice to him. Besides, he is younger than you are, and you should be nice to him anyway."

"Yes, ma'am," Jimmy grumbled. When his mother pulled his arm to return to their place in line, he sent a nasty look back in Eric's direction with his tongue stuck out and his eyes crossed before he quickly stepped back to walk beside his mother who had witnessed none of it.

Anna and Katrin had heard the exchange, but thought it was settled. They noticed hi grandmother Elsie was walking with difficulty so Anna went to her side. "Would an arm to hold onto be of help?"

Elsie smiled. "Yes, thank you, dear." She hooked her hand in Anna's bent elbow and they walked on toward the train they were to take.

"The man at the ticket booth said that it wouldn't be long before a new arrangement was made with the trains. Soon a traveler will get on a train in New York and not have to get off until he gets to Chicago," Anna explained. "Wouldn't that be nice if we could have done that for this trip?"

"That would be much easier," Elsie said with an attempt at a smile. "But I would like it if the ride was not so bumpy, and I worry when we sway from side to side. I feel like the train will tip over."

"Oh, dear. I don't think that would happen," Anna assured her.

"I'm afraid that the rocking just puts us to sleep," Katrin said. "I guess we're more tired than we thought from the voyage here."

The line slowed and Katrin found herself walking alongside Rose.

"I'm sorry my boy wasn't nicer to Eric back there," Rose said. "I hope he don't get his paw into trouble."

Katrin shook her head. "I'm sure he won't. Actually, we hoped Jimmy-Bob might ride with Eric once we got off the trains and traveled by coach. Eric is always looking for something to do, and he's chomping at the bit having to stay with his grandmother. Having another boy in the coach would be good."

Rose laughed. "Yes, I'd like that, too, but don't let my son hear you call him Jimmy-Bob. That's what we called him back home in Virginia, and I have to admit I use the full name only if I'm not happy about something he's done. He hates it when I do. You see, when we left to move north to New York after my husband got stationed there, all the kids made fun of him having two names. He insisted we call him plain Jimmy from now on."

"In my country boys have only one name with their family name," Katrin replied.

Rose paused to get a better grip of the coarse woven sack that she carried over her shoulder. "I wish I'd had time to sew on straps on this bag like you have," she admitted. "But at least I have a bag now. When the Yankee soldiers came through the woods toward our Virginia cabin, they were burning or stealing everything. We only had time to put a few things on the bed and pull up the corners of the quilt to carry it all."

"That must have been terribly frightening."

"It was—frightening to see them coming and frightening to see family and friends shot and unable to escape, their homes burned."

"You lived in the south so that was the Yankee soldiers from the north, right?"

Rose nodded her head in agreement. Jimmy, who had been walking close enough to hear their conversation, turned back to them. "Ma and I ran to the cave I used to play in. We hid there until the Blue Coats had gone on by."

"We might not be here if we hadn't hidden. I was so proud of Jimmy," Rose added with a smile for her son. She ruffled his hair with her hand. "He saved our lives that day. He knew right where we could hide. When we went back to the cabin after we thought it was safe, we found it burning. Our animals were all gone. With no home we just moved on from place to place to find food. So many folks had no homes left that it was hard. We had to hide during the day and move on at night. We didn't even know who to trust."

"They got Paw's unit and kept him a prisoner," Jimmy put in.

Rose put her arm around the boy and hugged him to her side. "We heard the news about Jethro from some soldiers who got away."

"They said Paw was still alive so we sure hoped he would be all right," Jimmy said.

"It wasn't easy to find where they'd taken him, but when we did, we tried to stay close by," Rose said. She slowly shook her head.

"I cannot imagine losing everything and not having anyone to help you."

"You know what I miss from the house that burned?"

Katrin saw tears in her eyes when she looked up at her. "I miss my Grandma's wood rocking chair. Grandpaw made it for her. I rocked Jimmy-Bob in it, and I rocked our sweet li'l Becky-Sue." She swiped at the tears on her cheeks with the sleeve of her dress. "Becky-Sue was just a babe when we had to go on the run. We didn't have no regular meals or even much good water to drink so I lost my milk. I…I couldn't keep my own little baby alive."

"I'm so sorry," Katrin said softly. She felt tears burn in her own eyes.

Rose swiped at her tears. "My goodness, how I'm going on about it all. I'm sorry to burden you with it all."

"I don't mind," Katrin told her. "Sometimes it feels good to talk about bad times."

Rose looked over at her. "Thank you."

"May I ask you a question?" Katrin dared to say.

Rose nodded with a bit of an encouraging smile.

"How…how did your husband end up in the Northern Army wearing a blue coat when they burned your cabin and took your husband prisoner?"

"Oh, that's easy. When the war was over, the prisoners was all given a choice. They was all free to go, so they could go back home down south if they wanted. They was also offered a place in their Army. With no cabin to go back to, Jethro decided that he would join up, and we would move to wherever they sent him and start over. When Jethro was told he would go west to man the forts out there, he jumped at the chance. The best part was that it turned out we got to go, too. The Army wants families to go with the soldiers. They opened the land out there for white folks to move in, and we don't have to pay for it."

"They've been nice to let us trail along with all the families."

Rose smiled. "There are more single soldiers than married ones. I'll bet they was right happy to have two single ladies come along."

Katrin laughed. "No, we're promised to the Oleson brothers. They are in the Dakota Territory already and waiting for us. We just have to find where they live and then we'll be married."

"It's a big country. I sure hope you find 'em."

Katrin frowned. She hadn't really thought about that. If the Dakota Territory were big, how would they ever find their husbands-to-be?

Katrin had never met a woman who had gone through so much on her own without a husband at her side to help. She hoped for that much courage should she need it in the future.

Sergeant McDougal was beside the car they were to occupy to help everyone on board. Another soldier with dirty gray pants and a newer blue jacket joined them. He lifted the burden of the sack from Rose's back and helped her up the steps onto the train. Jimmy jumped up ahead of them.

"This is my husband Jethro," Rose told Katrin over her shoulder as she climbed the steps with his help. Turning back to him at the top, she added, "This here is Miss Katrin."

"Howdy, ma'am. Pleasure to make your acquaintance," he said before turning and following his wife and son into the car.

"The pleasure is mine," Katrin called after him, stopping at an empty bench seat near the back of the car in a position similar to the seat she'd had on each of the previous trains.

Jethro went on down the aisle to help his wife and son into an empty seat toward the front. It didn't take long for the rest of the families to get aboard. They all busied themselves with stowing their bags and equipment on the overhead racks and then settled into their seats while their soldier husbands and fathers went back to report for duty loading the boxcars.

Adam was still occupied seeing that the horses got transferred so Anna helped settle Elsie and Eric several rows ahead of the seat she would share with her sister. Leaving their coats on their seats to save them, Katrin followed to help and introduced Anna to Rose and her family before they made their way back to their seat at the rear of the car.

Finally settled in their own seats, Katrin told Anna what Rose had said happened to them during the war. They agreed that it would be terrible to have no means of support, no food or home, and to have a dependent child. Anna shivered at the thought. How could she ever provide a good life for a child if she had nothing? What would she do if that happened to her?

Chapter 3

Transferring to the next train was apparently taking longer than expected so Anna left her seat to spend time with Elsie and Eric. Sergeant Tavis McDougal was quick to rise and turn back to the seat Anna had vacated. Grinning, because his lieutenant was still dealing with the horses in the boxcars and wouldn't be back for a while, he asked, "Ma'am, do you mind if I join you? Talking to someone besides the private would be most welcome."

Katrin glanced forward at Anna and wondered what her sister would think of the sergeant taking her place for a time. As suddenly as the thought entered her mind, she dismissed it. This was a new country, and they had agreed they would have to get used to new things.

"I do not mind at all," she said in her best English.

"I was so glad to hear that you ladies speak English. I heard you talking Norwegian with the lieutenant and I thought I was doomed, because English is the only language I speak. Well, that and a little Gaelic, but I don't expect you know how to speak that," he said with a laugh.

"No, I do not," Katrin admitted, returning his smile. "Once we knew we were coming to America, we worked on our English every moment we could. But we still make mistakes. You must tell me if I do. I want to learn to say things right."

"I'd think you say things right already, ma'am. You have a bonnie voice."

"Well, thank you, Sergeant McDougal. That is kind of you to say."

"Ma'am," the sergeant said, his brow knitted in a frown. "Did I hear rightly that you and your sister are going to the Dakota Territory to find the men you are promised to?"

Katrin nodded. "Yes, and I don't know how we'll find them. We were hoping another letter would arrive from them before we left, but it didn't. We haven't seen them in three years and we didn't see them often before that. I barely remember what they look like. They took turns coming to America so they could start a new life here. Their uncle wanted them to have Norwegian wives from back home so he chose us to come to America to be their wives."

The sergeant frowned and looked away for a few moments. Returning his gaze to meet hers, he shook his head slowly. "I beg your pardon, ma'am. I don't understand. What do you mean that an uncle chose you to be the brides? Doesn't a man in Norway pick his own bride over there? He has to let another man do it for him?"

"Their uncle, Ole Oleson, promised them he would send two brides after a year and so he sent us."

The sergeant slapped his hands on his thighs. "I've heard of such things, but I never met anyone who was a party to them before. I would want to pick my own bride—a woman I know and care for. I wouldn't want any uncle of mine picking her for me."

Katrin looked away. "It's difficult to understand an arranged marriage if you're not familiar with them. I know of several women who have come here to be brides to men that they really didn't know."

He shook his head. "You're right. I don't understand. But tell me this. What happens if you meet someone else that you would rather marry than these brothers who are somewhere out west in the Dakota Territory?"

Katrin looked at him as she tried to think of an answer. She could only shake her head. "I don't know what we would do then. We promised to marry them and they are expecting us to come. They will be looking for us, too."

Anna returned to her seat then, and the sergeant rose to give it to her.

"I hope you don't mind my talking with your sister. It helps pass the time, don't you know."

"I don't mind, Sergeant," she said with a smile for him as she sat beside her sister. "You have been so kind to us when you have so many other people to look after. We must thank you for all your help getting on and off these high train cars, too."

"It's my job to make sure all the families are made comfortable, but believe me, between trains, it's a job just to keep them together with all their bags and cases," he said with a grin.

"The lieutenant is lucky to have such a good man," Katrin told Anna.

He laughed. "Thank you. At least I get to be in here instead of trying to get frightened horses into a dark boxcar. I'd rather talk to you any time," he said, looking right at Katrin who laughed lightly at the thought. He nodded and resumed his seat in front of them.

Anna looked at the rosy red in her sister's cheeks and the broad smile on her face, and she began to worry. The private conversations with the sergeant had probably lasted long enough. It wouldn't do to have her sister get attracted to a soldier. It wouldn't do at all.

* * * *

Every train they had been traveling on stopped at regular intervals to take on water. The train ran on steam so without water, the train couldn't move. It didn't matter if they stopped during the day or in the dark of night, the procedure was the same. The train pulled up to the water tower slowly to get the tank lined up with the arm that swung down to deliver the water when it was right over the tank. When the tank was full, the arm was raised and the water stopped running.

This process, Eric thought each time it happened when he was awake, was not possible without him supervising. When the train slowly entered a station he checked out the window at his seat, and then told his grandmother he was going to his father's seat. He'd forgotten to tell her the first time.

"You need to go back to your seat and tell her you will be with me," his father said in no uncertain terms.

"But they'll finish before we get out there to watch," the boy complained.

"Then you had better run, but don't run into anyone else in the aisle."

Eric heaved a quick sigh and ran to do his father's bidding.

Anna had been watching this going on for a few stops and her curiosity was peaked. Grinning at the idea of joining them, she asked, "If I tell Katrin where I'm going, can I go, too? I have never seen this."

Adam laughed. "You are welcome to go."

Eric raced back down the aisle and Adam rose to take him to the door at the back of the car.

"I'm going to see what Eric is so excited about," Anna told Katrin. "I'll leave this with you," she added, putting her small bag on the seat beside her sister.

Hurrying to catch up, Anna got to the steps when Adam had just stepped down. He heard her behind him and turned. He raised his hands and laid them on each side of her waist, and when she'd wrapped her hands around his arms, he lifted her down to the platform. He didn't let her go right away. Standing inches apart, Adam smiled.

"Thank you for your help," Anna said.

"My pleasure," he replied.

"Father, come on. They've already started."

Adam chuckled and dropped his hands. "We're coming."

When Adam reached Eric, he lifted him up to sit on his shoulders. From that vantage point, he told Anna what the trainmen were doing as they delivered the water to the train.

"Look," Eric urged. "They must have the tank full. See the arm moving back up?"

"Yes. I'm so glad I came to see it for myself," Anna told him.

"Time to get back on the train," Adam said. "They're getting ready to go."

Back at the steps, Adam lifted Eric onto the top step. "Go let your grandmother know you're back on the train."

"All right, Father." He took a step toward the car door and then stepped back. "Thank you, Father. I'm glad you let Miss Anna come with us. She's never been on a train before either. She told me so when she stopped to talk to us."

Adam chuckled as he wrapped his hands around the sides of Anna's waist and lifted her onto the broad first step. Not letting go, he stepped up to face her.

"Thank you, Anna," he said softly.

She smiled. "Thank me for what?" she asked.

"For taking a caring interest in Eric and for all the times you have helped Elsie get from one train to the next. I don't know what we would do without you."

"I don't mind at all," she said with a smile.

The train lurched into motion and she was thrown against him. She uttered a little cry and grabbed his upper arms to feel safer on the step.

"Up you go," he said with a grin as he lifted her to the top step and then joined her there.

"You had me worried there. I didn't like standing at the edge of something moving so fast," she admitted.

"I wouldn't let anything bad happen to you, Anna."

She shook her head slowly. "No, I think that if it was at all within your power, you would not let anything bad happen to me. I thank you for that, too."

He glanced into the car through the window in the door and looked back at her. "We should go on in. They might be worried we didn't make it back on the train before it left the station."

"Yes, I wouldn't want them to worry."

Anna smiled as she turned out of his caring grip and walked on unsteady legs into the car. She sat down beside her sister and managed to not look at Adam when he sat down in his seat moments later. She could feel the heat still in her cheeks that rose when she had been standing with her body against his when the train started. She'd never felt that way just from being close to a man.

"Are you all right?" Katrin asked softly.

She nodded. "Yes, of course. I'm fine. Why?"

"Well, your face is pretty red."

"Oh," she replied as she covered her cheeks with her cool fingers. "It must be the wind while we were standing on the platform watching them fill the water tank."

Katrin looked out the window. "Oh, I hadn't noticed the wind, but it does feel cooler in here."

"Good thing we have our coats to put on for sleeping tonight."

* * * *

"Chicago's next," the conductor called from the rear door of the car. He paused a few moments as if waiting for questions and when there were none, he disappeared back into the next passenger car.

When Anna and Katrin heard they were nearing their destination, they made one last trip to the necessary at the opposite end of the car. It seemed that everyone else had thought that would be a good idea, too, so they had to wait in the line that formed in the aisle. But just standing for a while felt good after sitting most of the time for days.

Eric and Elsie had been ahead of them in the line. Coming back from their turn, the sisters stopped to talk as they had each time they passed. With each conversation they'd had, Anna thought Elsie looked more and more tired and not at all well, and she was worried about her. On this visit Katrin just uttered a few pleasantries and moved on to her seat. However, Anna perched on the edge of the seat beside Eric and asked Elsie how she was doing. She reached over Eric to lay her hand over Elsie's and felt it was cold.

"I'll be very glad to get off this rocking train," Elsie admitted in a weak voice.

"I'm afraid the next method of travel that we have will be no easier," Anna told her.

"Next we get to ride on wagons pulled by horses," Eric said with an eager grin. "I get to watch the horses."

"Do you like horses?" Anna asked him.

"Yes. When we get settled, Father said I can have a horse of my own. Then we can go riding together."

"I can see you are very excited about that."

"Yes, but Grandmother doesn't want to learn to ride. She says she's too old."

"That's right, dear. I'm not interested in riding a horse at all. That would be bumpier than this train," Elsie said. "I would rather ride in a well-spring carriage with thick padded seats." She smiled weakly at her grandson.

"That sounds lovely. I hope the wagons will be easier for you than this train, but I don't think they'll match a carriage, like you described, for comfort," Anna put in with a smile.

"We get to ride in the wagons, but Father gets to ride his horse. He brought it all the way from New York. Father says the Army will have horses for all his men who don't have their own when we get to the coach stop. After that the families will ride in the wagons with the bags and trunks and the men can ride their horses."

"The buildings are getting closer together and the streets are busier," Anna noted, looking out the window beyond Elsie. "It won't be long before we get to the Chicago station."

Elsie smiled at Eric. "And you can't wait to see all the horses that the soldiers will have, can you?"

"I wish I could ride a horse, too, and not ride in the wagon," he said with a glance at his grandmother.

"But I would be lonesome without you to keep me company," Elsie admitted with a smile.

Eric looked at Anna. "You could sit with her, couldn't you, Miss Anna? Then I could ride a horse."

"I would be happy to if they let me," Anna said. "That would make our travel very pleasant if I have your grandmother to talk to. But, you see, my sister and I are not certain how we will travel beyond Chicago."

"I bet there will be room for you to go with us," Eric said.

"That would be wonderful, but we'll have to wait and see. Your father said he would tell us what we need to do to arrange for our own travel."

"Do you think the horses are at the station already?" Eric asked, returning the conversation to his favorite subject.

"I don't know, but if the horses are for the soldiers in the Army, I wouldn't count on there being one for you, Eric. You father is probably thinking that you would get to ride one after you're settled in Dakota Territory."

The smile flew from Eric's face. "Yes, I know. I just wish I could ride one now."

Anna felt the train slowing and glanced out the window to see other trains and other tracks close by. "We must be coming into the station. I should get back to my seat and check that I have everything in my bag."

"Thank you for stopping by," Elsie said with a smile. "I've enjoyed talking about places we know in Norway with you on your other visits."

"My pleasure." She looked down at Eric seated between them. "Thank you for sharing your seat."

The boy laughed as she rose and headed back down the aisle. Her gaze rose to the back of the car where she saw the lieutenant watching her. When their gazes met, he smiled warmly. Feeling some heat rising in her cheeks, she looked across the aisle at her own seat. She wasn't surprised to see the sergeant sitting there again. He took advantage of her absence every time so he could sit beside Katrin. Her sister had told her that they talked about everything from being in the Army to his life before the war in Ohio.

"My English is much better, because we always talk in English," Katrin had bragged just that morning with a smile. But her smile had quickly disappeared as she looked up at Anna. "He's been so kind. You don't think that the Oleson brothers would mind that we spend time each day talking?" she added softly.

Anna smiled and patted the hand that Katrin had placed on her arm. "These soldiers have made our journey much easier so far. I think the Oleson brothers would thank them for their help and friendship."

But it wasn't Adam's help that Anna was thinking about, it was the way he made her feel. She pressed her lips together between her teeth and frowned. That was not something the Oleson brothers would thank him for. She watched out the window at all the new sights as they came into another city larger than any they had seen since leaving New York City. It wasn't long before the train slowed to a stop.

* * * *

Arriving in Chicago, the passengers all exited the cars and stood with their bags and cases on the platform waiting for orders of where to go next. As everyone was assembling, the stationmaster sought out Lieutenant Johnson. "I have good news," he said, waving a piece of paper as he approached. "The track to St. Paul, Minnesota, has been completed. We have this telegram for you that orders you to continue on there by train."

The lieutenant took the telegram and opened it to read it all. "Hold it, men," he shouted to stop the ones who had begun to move down the platform. "Remain where you are. Our orders have changed. Another train will take us to St. Paul."

A few in the crowd cheered. Most just wondered out loud what was going on. Following the new orders, the soldiers and their families stayed close on the platform with their cases and bags beside them.

"But, aren't the wagons and horses waiting for us here?" the sergeant asked.

The lieutenant shrugged. "They must have transferred that order to St. Paul."

"Some of the horses the Army sent for you are already here," the stationmaster told them. "They are loading them into boxcars for your trip. We'll have to wait until the ones on this train have been transferred before it can leave."

"Where do we all go from here?"

"The train for St. Paul is on Track Four, Lieutenant," the stationmaster said.

"If there aren't enough horses here, I hope they round up more in St. Paul before we get there. I don't want to wait for them once we get there," the lieutenant said. "Can you send a telegraph to tell them that?"

The stationmaster promised he would. The lieutenant thanked him and put the order papers in the pack he carried on his belt before he turned back to his men to explain the orders more fully. "Can you tell me how long it will take us to get to St. Paul?"

"Your travel time there could be as little as thirty hours if all goes well," the stationmaster replied. "You'll be among the first to ride the new rails," he added with a broad and proud grin.

"Sergeant, tell the families to gather their things. We have another train to find on Track Four. And be sure all the trunks and cases make the change. Take a couple men with you to check on them. We won't be coming back to get something left behind."

The sergeant explained the change of trains to the men and their families and pointed them toward Track Four while the lieutenant found Elsie and Eric to explain it to them himself. From there he went to supervise moving the horses they already had with them and adding the new ones waiting for them here.

"What a difference from the weeks it took Lars and Ingor to cover the same distance on horseback," Anna said as she helped Katrin lift the strap of her larger sack onto her shoulder.

"I wasn't looking forward to walking in these stiff shoes," Katrin confessed. "I'm glad we get to ride longer."

The sergeant stepped up behind Katrin. "Do you ladies need help with your bags?"

Katrin's face lit up with a smile for him. "Thank you, but no. They are easy to carry."

"This train will only take us to St. Paul. That means we have Minnesota to cross after we get off in St. Paul, doesn't it?" Anna asked.

"Right you are," the sergeant told her.

"But Minnesota can't be too big, can it?" Katrin asked.

"Just a few days more on the train and we'll get there," the sergeant said with a grin. "But I would enjoy it while you have it." He touched the tip of his hat brim with his fingers and walked on to see if he could be of help to anyone else.

"A few more days? It can't take that long, can it?" Katrin asked Anna. "I'm tired of sitting."

Anna shrugged. "We'll have to wait and see, but you can't have it both ways. You can't avoid walking in stiff shoes and not want to sit at the same time."

Katrin sighed and smiled. "I think you're right, and I would rather be sitting in these padded seats than walking."

Anna slung her large bag strap over her shoulder. "Come on. We have to stay with the other Army passengers, but keep watching for the ticket office. We need to buy two tickets to St. Paul."

They fell in line with the soldiers with families who carried their goods from the one track to the other. They passed the boxcar where soldiers helping the sergeant were unloading the trunks and large suitcases belonging to the soldiers' families. They piled them on four-wheeled carts for the move to the next train.

Anna and Katrin made the train change easily even with the purchase of tickets for this part of the trip. They even selected some food items from the station vendors that would last a few days and made the purchases along with the rest of the families. They also had to believe it would be safe because the only alternative was to starve.

Being more familiar with train travel and knowing what to expect on the journey ahead of them made such a huge difference.

Worrying less, they were able to enjoy the sights and sounds around them. Everything was new to them. They had never ridden a train before this trip and they found themselves in a station with several trains lined up on parallel tracks. They had never traveled over such great distances, or seen so many people who spoke different languages, or gone through such big cities as New York or Chicago.

And they had never been solely responsible for their own situation before. The fact that they were succeeding in finding their way across the vast country, even with the soldiers' help, gave them confidence that they would succeed in their search for the Oleson brothers once they reached their destination.

Like the other passengers, Anna and Katrin were each happy to postpone riding in coaches or covered wagons. In the absence of the well-sprung carriage she would prefer, so was Elsie. "Would you like to sit closer to us and the lieutenant," Anna asked Elsie as they waited in line to board the last train they would ride in.

"Thank you, my dear, but I'd like to be closer to the necessary. I have too much trouble walking in the rocking car," she explained. "I'm always grabbing onto the back of the seat or even someone's shoulder to keep my balance."

"We'll still stop and chat when we pass," Anna promised. She didn't volunteer to sit forward farther, because she knew that both she and Katrin enjoyed sitting near the lieutenant and the sergeant with whom they often talked now despite Anna's former thoughts of ending the conversations.

The lieutenant sent Eric on ahead to find an empty seat as he took his mother-in-law's arm to help her forward. As soon as they were settled, he returned to put his saddlebags on the seat, opposite where Anna and Katrin sat, and went back outside. The sergeant and the same private, who sat beside him before, appeared to put their rifles and bags on the shelf over the seat ahead of the sister's. They dropped their overcoats on the seats. When they turned back to leave the car, Katrin asked them how much longer the wait would be before the train started moving.

"We have to load the horses that were waiting for us here. They're not at all happy about getting into a boxcar."

"You will be careful, won't you?" Katrin asked.

The sergeant gave her a broad grin and touched the brim of his hat in a salute. "Thank you, ma'am. I'll be doing exactly that."

The grin on Katrin's face was as broad as his as she watched him leave the car. Anna saw the matching grins and hoped that Katrin and the sergeant were not becoming too well acquainted with each other. The soldiers had helped them more that she could have imagined, but they were on a journey to meet their husbands. A case of heartache over a soldier they had met on the journey would make it extremely difficult when they got there. They both should remember that.

In the absence of help, Anna and Katrin managed to get their own bags up on the shelf over their seats and sat down to clear the aisle so the other passengers could pass more easily. They waited over an hour when their curiosity won and they stepped to the back end of the car and looked out the door to see down the platform.

"They're still loading the horses," Katrin said.

"Eric would love to see this, but they are almost done."

Standing on the bottom step to the car and holding onto vertical bars, they watched as the last three horses were walked up the ramp into one of the boxcars.

"The sergeant was right about them not wanting to go inside," Anna noted when the last horse was aboard. "I didn't see one go willingly."

Katrin laughed. "It is probably their first ride on a train, too."

"I think you're right." Anna smiled at her sister. It was so nice to hear her make a jest instead of complaining or worrying.

After the last horse was stabled in the boxcar, the soldiers slid the door shut and pulled back the ramp. They left the rest to the station workers while they cleaned up the best they could at the horse trough filled with water in the now empty corral. Retrieving their jackets from the fence rail, they pulled them on and headed for the passenger cars. Anna and Katrin returned to their seats from their spot in the doorway. Once the soldiers were on board and the lieutenant and the sergeant had taken a count of the men, the conductor shouted to the engineer from the steps, and the train finally began to move.

Rationing the food they had purchased in the station, the sisters ate a modest supper. The lieutenant walked forward to check on his family, but soon returned to his seat with a smile on his face.

"That boy is so excited about seeing the horses that it might be a struggle to get him to sleep inside in a bed instead of in the corral with the mounts," Adam told Anna.

"He's going to be an eager student when you teach him to ride."

"I hope he's that eager to find a place in a school there. I don't know what arrangements have been made at the fort for the children."

Anna smiled. "If I had stayed in Norway, I was going to be a teacher for the children."

"That's wonderful," Adam replied. "If they have no classes arranged for the children, would you consider organizing them?"

"I would like that," Anna said with a smile that quickly disappeared. "Oh, but I don't know where I will be living. If whichever Mr. Oleson I am to marry is not living near the fort, I won't be there to hold any classes."

"Yes, of course," Adam said, nodding, a frown on his face. "I didn't think of that." Still frowning, he looked over at Anna. "Wait a minute." He turned in his seat so his feet were planted in the aisle and he was facing her. "What did you just say? 'Whichever Mr. Oleson'? Don't you even know which brother you will marry?"

Anna shook her head and looked down at her hands that were clutched together in her lap. She didn't want to think of that now. When she was talking to Adam, she didn't like to think of the Oleson brothers at all. "No, we don't." She cleared her throat. "We didn't ever meet them in Norway. I mean we had seen them and knew who they were. In a town like ours everyone knew who everyone was, but we never spoke to them."

Adam frowned and leaned forward with his elbows on his thighs. "I don't understand. You're going to marry them and you have never talked to them? They never proposed to you?"

She shook her head and couldn't raise her gaze to meet his. "No, but it is all arranged. We each will marry the one that we feel most comfortable with just as they will want the one of us that seems good for them."

Adam laved his face with his hands and looked at her again. "I don't know how you can do it. I could not marry a woman that I did not love."

Tears burned at the backs of Anna's eyes when she thought of not marrying for love, but she said nothing.

"When you get to the Dakota Territory, you can't just go live with them. You will have to marry right away. You will have no time to fall in love with either one of the brothers."

Anna wished he would stop talking about it. "No, I don't imagine we will, and that is the sad part of our promise. But, we don't always get what we wish for."

Unable to talk any more past the lump growing in her throat, she leaned her head back against the seat and closed her eyes to end the conversation. It was too painful to continue.

Chapter 4

Just before dark, the train stopped at a station where the sisters saw a man waiting with a small suitcase. The station house behind him was only partially finished. The wooded walls were framed in and the roof was on, but no more had been done. Stacks of planks dotted the platform along the wall. At the end of the platform, the supports for the water tank were completed, and the construction of the water tank had been begun. A few buildings lined the street of the small town beyond the station, but the only activity they could see was at the saloon.

The man got on the train in one of the cars behind theirs, but the train didn't leave right away. The passengers could hear other men shouting to the conductor from the platform, but they couldn't make out what they were saying. They saw the conductor meeting one of the train engineers on the platform. They held an animated conversation with their arms gesturing and their heads shaking. Another engineer joined them, but just for a minute or so. Then they went back to where they belonged. Several minutes later, the train pulled out of the station. The darkness and the car rocking soon put the passengers to sleep. Leaning against their small bags as if they were pillows, the sisters quickly followed suit.

Sometime during the night the train began to slow down. The changes in the sounds and the rhythm of the movement woke the sisters. Leaning over Katrin to look out the window, Anna asked, "What's happening? Can you see anything?"

"I think we're stopping, so it must be another station. Could it be St. Paul so soon?"

Lieutenant Johnson rose. "I see nothing but trees on my side. Can you see why we are stopping?" He leaned over a bit beside them to see out the window on their side. "No, too dark to tell what's going on out there." He tapped the sergeant, who had been looking out his window, on the shoulder. "Let's find out."

With the sergeant following him, Adam left the car. It didn't take long before everyone was awake and asking why they had stopped. Several of the soldiers went outside to see for themselves while the families remained in their seats, trying to see out their windows.

The lieutenant came back several minutes later with his men. "Sorry, folks," he announced to the whole car. "It seems we've run out of water for the engine. They can't generate steam to run the train without water." He shook his head. "They finished laying the track we're on, but they haven't finished the stations. There was no water in the tower at the last one where we stopped. So feel free to move about and exercise your legs. Stay inside for safety in the dark, though. This train is not going anywhere until they find water, and because we're between stations, that can't happen until daylight."

Groans and complaints were heard all up and down the car, but since it was dark out, no one moved far from their seats. Most tried to sleep again. However, when the sun began to rise and the visibility improved outside, the passengers took advantage of the stop and stepped off the train. Anna and Katrin, their small bags in hand as usual, joined the line next to Eric and Elsie.

The sergeant was on the ground helping the ladies down from the high step and he took Eric's hand. Anna turned to take Eric's other hand as he gleefully jumped down. She was comforted to see the sergeant help Elsie to the ground by cradling her in his arms and lifting her down rather than expecting her to step down.

"Oh, my, we're up so high," Elsie said, looking down from the raised gravel bed on which the track had been laid.

"You'd better take Grandma's hand instead of mine," Eric told Anna.

"What a gentleman," Anna said with a warm smile. "I think you're right."

Anna turned back to help Elsie walk over the stones, and the three of them made their way down to the tall grass where the slope was more gentle. In the distance they could see the sun reflected on the surface of a lake.

"What a beautiful spot," Anna said.

"I wonder if there are fish in that lake," Eric asked.

"I'll bet there are. Do you like to fish?" Katrin asked.

He shrugged with one shoulder. "Never got a chance to. Father didn't get home much and Grandmother didn't know how."

"Adam says the fort is close by the Red River. I bet he'll teach you how to fish when we get there," Elsie put in.

"If he has the time. I heard the men talking when the train was stopped. They said they had a lot of Indians to shoot first," Eric replied.

Anna gasped. "Oh, I hope not," she said softly.

Eric had taken to picking up small stones and throwing them into the field between the train and the lake where the grasses that grew there were dotted with spring flowers in bloom. "Hey, look," he said, stopping and pointing into the field. "Where are those men going?"

The trio watched and soon realized that railroad men were heading to the lake they could see beyond the high grass. Word soon spread that they were going after water for the train. The laborious job of carrying water by the pail-full from lake to the engine was neither quick nor easy, even with the soldiers' help.

"Do they have to do it this way?" Eric asked. "It's taking so long."

"Yes, but you know normally water would be put in the train from the overhead tank at a station like they did when I watched them with you and your father," Anna told him. "We often stopped for people and water at the same time before now. But when we picked up the man at that new station late last night, the sergeant said the tower for the water wasn't finished so it wasn't filled yet. They couldn't get any water there."

Eric nodded. "They should finish it. This way is slower."

"Yes. Now the men have to hand the pails up to one of the engineers who is standing on top of the tank where he can pour them in."

"Look, more soldiers have joined in to help. They're passing the pails of water from one man to the next, but they don't have very many pails."

"It is a slow process."

"But in the meantime we get to sit in the fresh air where we can see the sun reflected on the lake and a field of flowers in many colors. This is much more pleasant than sitting on that bumpy train," Elsie said.

"It is nice," Anna agreed.

While the passengers waited, most ate what they had for breakfast outdoors on the grass. Anna noticed that Katrin was happily talking with two of the Army wives. Keeping an eye on Eric who was still throwing small rocks into the field, Anna pulled up some of the long grass growing beside where they sat and tried to braid it.

Eric stopped throwing to watch as she fed new blades into the braid that was getting longer. "I wonder, could you make a basket?"

"What?" Anna asked.

"The grass. Can you make a basket with it?"

"Let's give it a try." Anna braided and wove the grass that Elsie and Eric handed her, but she couldn't get the strands to stay in the basket form. She was unable to hold all the loose ends and the braids kept popping free. She finally managed a basket big enough to put over Eric's thumb by knotting the ends of the green pliable grass. They laughed about her attempts.

"I wish I could go see the horses," Eric said as he looked back toward the boxcars that were behind the passenger cars.

"You'll see them soon enough, but look, now you can see the soldiers carrying pails of water to the box cars. They must have run out of water for the horses, too. See them handing the full pails up to men inside?"

Eric nodded. "Couldn't I just run take a peek?" he asked as he inched away toward the boxcar.

"No, you can't," Anna said. "Your father said to stay with your grandmother, but you'll get to see the horses in St. Paul."

His face was twisted in an unhappy look, but he remained where he was.

The train's whistle blew just then. Not expecting the loud sound so close to them, everyone jumped. A few cried out and then everyone laughed.

"That means they have the steam up. We need to get back on the train. Help your grandmother up, please," Anna said. Already experienced beyond his years, he leaned over to take a hold of her upper arm and lift while Anna did the same with her other arm. Elsie was so thin that lifting her was no problem.

"Thank you both," Elsie said once she was standing. "I know Adam is anxious to get going again," she said of her son-in-law. "But I must say, this has been a very pleasant break."

"It was like a picnic," Eric added. "And I like picnics."

Anna offered her arm for Elsie to hold as they walked to the steps to their car. The sergeant was stationed there to help folks back onto the train.

"Ready for your ride up the steps?" he asked Elsie with a grin.

"Oh, Sergeant," she teased. "It has been decades since I was in the arms of such a handsome man."

Laughing at her comment, the sergeant very gently lifted Elsie up onto the car. Once inside Anna walked with her and Eric to their seat and waited for them to get settled. With a promise to stop by their seat later, she went back to her own seat.

Already there, Katrin was watching out her window as the sergeant helped the last of the passengers climb on board. "He is so nice and such a big help."

"I'm sure he was told to help," Anna guessed, not trying to be unkind.

"I don't think so. The lieutenant wasn't here to tell him. He's just like that."

"He does manage to keep everything going smoothly."

Katrin leaned closer and added in a whisper, "I think being so kind may be why he doesn't like being in the Army. He'd rather be farming."

"He told you he doesn't like being a soldier?" Anna asked with surprise.

"Shh." Katrin looked around. "Don't let anyone hear you. I don't want to get him in trouble." She paused while a soldier walked past to his seat ahead. "He has six months left to serve and then he wants to homestead. He wants to homestead on the free land in Dakota Territory like Lars and Ingor Oleson must have done by now."

"It would be nice to have neighbors that we know," Anna said. A glance at her sister left her wondering why that idea made her frown.

The lieutenant jumped up on the steps into the car and the

sergeant came in right behind him. "Take a count and if everyone is here, signal the conductor on the car behind us. We're ready to leave."

The sergeant did as he was ordered and leaned out the door to wave at the conductor who was watching for his signal. With a long blast on the whistle, the train slowly began to move again.

* * * *

Anna put the book she had been reading back into her small bag and saw the book of short stories there. She looked forward to see that Elsie's head was leaning against the window. She was probably asleep and that meant Eric would be bored with nothing to do and no one to talk to. She took the small tome of stories and turned to her sister.

"I'm going to keep Eric company while Elsie is asleep. I'll leave this with you," Anna said, handing Katrin her small bag. She put it on top of her own that sat between her feet and wall at the end of their seat.

Katrin watched her sister as she rose and walked up the aisle to sit beside Eric. She saw Anna lean over to talk to him and then saw him stand so Anna could sit down. He then sat on her lap. Katrin smiled. Her sister really enjoyed spending time with Eric. She glanced at the lieutenant who was going through papers that he carried in the pack at his waist.

She grinned more broadly when the sergeant glanced at her over his shoulder. He pointed to the empty seat beside her and she nodded. Anna would be gone for a while and she would like to have the sergeant come talk with her.

He rose and lowered himself into the seat beside her. A large man, he filled the seat. She slid a bit toward the window to give him all the room he wanted.

"Your sister is good to keep Eric company," he said in a low voice.

She liked that he could be quiet though she understood that he probably just didn't want the lieutenant to hear their conversation.

"He's a good little boy. She has always enjoyed being around children. She wanted to be a teacher if we had stayed in Norway."

"What about you? What did you want to do?"

Katrin shrugged. "I don't think I'd be a good teacher for lots of children. I want mine just one at a time," she said with a laugh. Realizing how personal a statement that was, she felt heat rise into her cheeks.

"I think you would make a beautiful mother."

She looked up to see the sweet smile on his face and felt her flesh rise in bumps on her arms. "Thank you, but you shouldn't say such things to me." She crossed her arms over her chest and rubbed her upper arms to stop the feeling in them.

"How can I not? Your pale hair, your blue eyes, and your skin as smooth as china—I like looking at you and talking with you."

"I like talking to you, too," she admitted, her hands grasping her upper arms. "Tell me more about Glasgow and what it was like living there."

"It's been ten years since I've been there," he admitted. He turned slightly in his seat to face her and crossed his arms, too. Their fingers rested against each other.

"We shouldn't..." she began.

He separated two fingers and squeezed one of hers to hold it. He glanced forward in the car to see that Anna was still reading to Eric. He looked back at Katrin and smiled. "Whatever you want," he said, not moving his hand from hers.

She looked at their fingers entwined together and up at him. She smiled tentatively, but she didn't move hers away.

He grinned. "As I was saying, I was just a boy in Glasgow. I remember getting into a lot of mischief playing in walled walkways and narrow roads that turned through the city. When I got lucky, I used to hold a horse's reins for gentlemen while they went inside somewhere. They would toss me a coin when they came out."

"I knew it. You were helping people even when you were a boy."

He shook his head. "No, lass, I was trying to earn money. I saved every coin I made and bought passage to America when I was eighteen. My ma had too many mouths to feed and gave me her blessings. I haven't seen her since."

"Do you write to her? Have you heard from her?"

He stroked her fingers with the back of his. "I write, but I don't know if she ever gets them. She's never written back, but she couldn't read or write so unless one of my brothers or sisters read the letter, she wouldn't know what it said."

"It must be hard not knowing, but I think she must have gotten the letter and had them read to her. She must be very proud of you."

He smiled and glanced forward again. "My time here is gone. Here comes your sister," he said. He sat up straighter and uncrossed his arms.

Katrin's fingers felt cold without his beside them. "Thank you for talking to me while she was gone."

"You wouldn't mind if I came again?" he asked.

"You know I would like that," she admitted.

The sergeant smiled and rose from the seat. He stepped back and allowed Anna to sit down beside her sister. "Ma'am," he said with a touch of his fingers to the brim of his hat. Once she was seated, he stepped forward and sat back in his own seat.

* * * *

After the train from Chicago pulled into the St. Paul station, pandemonium reigned. All the soldiers and their families had to get off the train and claim the baggage that had been stored in the boxcar. Children were crying, and mothers were becoming frantic at keeping track of them and all their goods, because, at the same time, about half of the soldiers had to report for the duty of unloading the horses. The horses were just as shy about coming out into the sunlight as they had been going in. Once the horses were out, the men had to carry the saddles and other tack out to the corral where the horses were kept for the time being.

Once all that was done, all the people and baggage had to be transported in wagons to the Mississippi River landing. They soon discovered that there were more people and bags than would fit the number of wagons available, so two trips had to be made. All of this took time.

Not knowing what they should do to arrange for the next step in their journey, Anna and Katrin were relieved when the lieutenant told them to stay with the families. "You won't need to worry about a ticket here. Just stay with us until you get to the coach stop. You can settle your fares to the Territory then."

The sisters had gotten separated from Eric and Elsie. The soldiers must have made sure the two of them got to the crossing at the head of the line. Anna felt badly that she wasn't nearby to help. Now, with so many people milling about, she couldn't even see them in the crowd.

Once at the river crossing, which thankfully wasn't too far from the station, the travelers had to ride on pontoon boats to cross. Anna and Katrin waited in line with their bags as the soldiers loaded the boats with as many people and goods as each would hold.

"Once you start across stand still where you are," a soldier warned as their pontoon was pushed off from the shore.

"I can see that getting a place in the middle and not moving would be best," Anna said.

"Especially since we don't know how to swim," Katrin remarked.

They looked back to see the soldiers having a hard time getting a horse to settle down on the pontoon behind theirs.

"I think the people are following orders not to move around, but getting the horses to remain in one place is not easy."

"But if they fall in, they can swim," Katrin added.

Their pontoon landed without incident and the passengers stepped up onto the short pier. Anna looked over where the soldiers and families were gathering after the crossing.

"Have you seen the lieutenant's family?" Anna asked, looking around at the people and piles of goods. "I'm afraid I lost track of them while we waited for the coaches to return to take more of us to this landing. I know they got a ride with the others on the earlier ones."

"Tavis said they already went across the river," Katrin told her. "The lieutenant went with them, and he must have made sure they were all right on the other side. I saw him come back on an empty pontoon."

"I'm sure he wanted to be back to see that all the rest crossed all right."

Anna shielded her eyes from the sun with her raised hand and searched for them all over the landing site. "I should be there to help her," Anna said. "Adam has done so much for us. He had already arranged for us to travel with his family when I asked if we might join them. He even talked to the wagon master who came to the station from the coach stop to arrange everything. Adam made sure that he knew we were traveling with his family."

"That's good and I do appreciate all he's done for us. He certainly has made our journey easier, but his family can manage without you over there. You're not their family, Anna."

Anna slowly lowered her arm and looked at Katrin. "I know," she said softly. "But I wish I was."

Katrin put her arm around her waist in a caring hug. "I thought so. Now I know that neither one of us wants to marry one of the Oleson brothers. What are we ever going to do?"

"I wish I knew," Anna replied. "But I don't."

Once across the river, transporting all the people and horses to the coach stop was not a quick task. Walking up the shore from the pontoon landing, the sisters saw a number of empty wagons were lined up on a road that ran along the river. They didn't have cloth stretched over the tops as Ingor described in his letter, and they could only hope it didn't rain if they had to ride in them.

At Anna's urging, the sisters located Elsie and Eric and sat with them while they waited for their assigned place in the wagons.

"The wagons are lined up like the railroad cars in trains," Eric said.

"They just don't ride on rails," Anna replied with a smile. "But they're still called wagon trains."

The efficient sergeant and other soldiers helped load people and goods on the waiting wagons. They didn't have far to go in them. The coach stop was their next destination, but getting all the people, trunks, other goods, and horses transported was not so easy.

Before leaving the corral at the train station, the horses had been bridled with hand-knotted rope and tied together into groups of three or four. The tethered horses made it across the river on the pontoons and now they were tied behind the wagons where metal rings had been attached for that purpose. Soldiers were riding bare back on a few others. The soldiers who had brought saddles west were riding their saddled mounts. All the horses were very frisky at first after being cooped up for so many days in the railroad car but soon settled down.

Since the wagon master had been told that Anna and Katrin were traveling with the lieutenant's family, they were assigned to the same wagon. Climbing aboard was not easy for Elsie, or any woman, because of the long skirts they had to contend with. They had to rely on the sergeant to help them up. Anna couldn't help but notice that every time the sergeant and Katrin were together, they whispered to each other and invariably laughed together. She could see they were coming to care for each other. She could only hope it didn't affect how Katrin thought about the Oleson brother she would marry. But all she had to do was think about how she felt about Adam. She knew then that it would.

Once in the wagon they sat on bench seats built in along the sides like in the wagons that took them to the train station from the Castle Garden in New York City. There were no seat cushions or padding of any kind. The back of the seat was the top horizontal plank of the side of the wagon. The seats were not designed for comfort.

"They can't mean to make us ride like this all the way across Minnesota," Elsie said as she tried to get comfortable on the bare plank.

"I hope they don't," Anna put in. "I should have asked about what the families were going to do. We might have found more comfortable transportation."

"This seat is hard," Eric soon complained as soon as the wagon began to move.

"These should help some," Anna said. She and Katrin took their larger fabric bags with the quilts packed in them and their coats and spread them on the seat so the four of them would have a more padded ride. Others around them quickly did the same with coats or shawls or whatever they had.

"That's better, isn't it, Eric? Yes, this is much better," Elsie said with a smile that the sisters were happy to see on her face. "But whatever you have in these will need a press, and you may never get the wrinkles out if this ride is long."

But the sisters didn't think of what the weight was doing to the dresses they brought to wear for their wedding because they could see that the ride was still too jarring for Elsie. "I wish I could do more to make you comfortable," Anna told her.

"Thank you both. Adam said this probably wasn't a good idea for me to travel all this way at my age, but I couldn't leave Eric alone to find his way with his father so busy with his men. I don't know how he would have managed. Besides, I have no family left back east so I didn't want to stay there all alone. I wanted to go with Adam and Eric."

"Now that we know we are to be traveling together the remainder of the trip, please tell us if we can be of help to you," Anna offered. "The lieutenant has been so good to us. I don't think we would have gotten this far in just a few weeks without his direction."

"We can watch Eric anytime you need help or if you want a rest," Katrin added.

Anna looked at Eric who had given up sitting on the seat and was standing at the front of the wagon, hanging on to the back of the driver's seat and watching the horses. "He does like horses. He's happy even watching them from behind."

The women laughed.

The ride in the open wagons thankfully turned out to be only long enough to get them to the coach stop west of the city. Soldiers helped move their families, bags, and trunks to empty the wagons. Following the sergeant's orders, all the people headed for the wooden building where they learned that they would be staying the night. Once all the wagons were empty, the freight company wagon drivers wasted no time. They turned the teams around and headed right back to the train station.

"Look at all the horses," Eric cried when he noticed the corral on the other side of the building where the horses were being led. He took off at a run, slid to a stop at the fence, and climbed up to stand on the middle horizontal post while holding the top one. His rapid movement so close by had startled the horses. They pranced to the far side of their fenced enclosure.

Adam, who had just been coming to check on his family, quickly caught up with him in a few long strides. "Slow down there, son," he said. "Horses don't like quick movement around them."

"Oh, I'm sorry," Eric said though he didn't climb down. "I didn't mean to scare them."

"I know you didn't. Just remember to move more slowly next time you're around them. They don't like surprises."

Eric nodded. "Where is your horse?" he asked, looking around to see one he recognized.

"He's somewhere in there with the rest. We have to sort them all out in the morning."

"Then each of the soldiers will have a horse to ride."

"That's the way it should be. We need a horse for each of my men, but there aren't enough here yet. It will take a while to locate more around here that the Army can buy for them." He lifted the boy from the rail and set him down facing the building. "You let us finish with the horses and go see if you can be a help to the ladies."

"Aw, do I have to?"

His father raised an eyebrow and stared at him silently.

"Yes, Father," he finally agreed without his father saying another word on the subject. Eric kicked at the dirt and turned to go back.

Adam stopped him with a gentle hand on his shoulder. He knelt down so his head was at Eric's level. "They need your help, son. You're a big boy now, and you can do a lot for them."

"I don't mind helping Grandma and Miss Anna, too. She's nice and I like her, don't you?"

Adam smiled. "Yes, son, I…I think she's very nice, too."

Agreed and understanding that his father had to work, Eric ran toward the others still making their way into the wood frame structure. He slid to a halt beside Anna.

"Papa said they have to sort out the horses in the morning. He said I could watch them then, but I can't move too fast. Horses don't like that," Eric announced.

"That's an important thing to remember, so I'm glad that you listened to your father. You can learn a lot from him," Anna told him.

"He's got his own horse, but I couldn't find him with all the others. I'll look again when I'm done helping you."

Anna smiled. "I think that would be fine. We can use your help now, and you'll get to see where we are staying tonight. We get to sleep in a real bed."

Chapter 5

When it was their turn to enter the post house, the sisters saw there were four rooms inside. A large center one had a fireplace at the back where they could smell that a large pot of beans was slow cooking. The rest of this room had several long tables with stools lining both sides of each one. Another small room off the back, not far from the fireplace, was where the couple running the stop slept.

Just inside the front door, the pile of bags and trunks grew and the families entered and set down their burdens as soon as possible.

"Men in there," the sergeant called out, pointing to a large room on one side. "And women and children in there," he added, pointing to one on the opposite side. The line split as the men and women went to their own rooms.

Wood-framed beds with straw mattresses lying on cross-tied ropes filled each of the rooms, leaving little room to walk between them. Doors in the back were open for air and several outhouses could be seen not far out that way.

Selecting four beds close to each other in the back corner, they put their bags under them.

"I'm going to take a rest," Elsie told them as she lay down on one of the beds. "I'll keep watch on everything."

Anna smiled, knowing what would happen. Elsie's eyes floated shut as soon as her head reached the pillow. A little sleep on a real mattress was just what the elderly woman needed. Confident that the room of soldier's wives and children would not disturb their things, the sisters left their bags and went out the back door with Eric to take care of personal needs. From there Eric was given permission to go watch the horses again with the other boys doing the same. He promised to walk and not run there and to stay out of the corral.

Behind the building the women saw several wooden washtubs. Anna and Katrin quickly agreed that the best part of the coach stop was the warm water available in the tubs that had been sitting in the sun all day. Carrying a pail-full inside where they had a little privacy, they washed up for the first time since leaving the ship from Norway. They longed for a tub they could sink into, but knew it wasn't to be. With no screens for privacy, they did the best they could to get clean and then put on clean clothes. Most women around them were doing the same thing. When Elsie woke after her nap, she did, too.

Though it was nearly time for supper when they finished, many of the women, including Anna and Katrin, washed out the clothes they had worn on the trip and hung them over fence rails outside to dry. Feeling clean and fresh for the first time in weeks, when the dinner bell rang, the sisters and Adam's family joined the others in the main room.

Dinner and breakfast the next morning came from the huge cast iron bean pot hanging in the fireplace. The diners tore apart freshly baked loaves of bread for dinner and washed it down with cold well water. Breakfast had the addition of fried eggs and freshly baked biscuits. The coffee they served with it was watered down, but it was a treat after not having any in weeks. The travelers all commented that the food was most welcome, even if a little undercooked. Most had not had so much food at one time since their journey began.

Anna noticed that Elsie looked better after a good night's sleep and filling meals. After breakfast, she asked Anna and Katrin to keep an eye on Eric. "I didn't want to sleep late and miss breakfast, but I do want to take a nap in a bed again while I have the chance," she said before heading back to the ladies' bedroom.

"We're happy to watch him, and we all know where he'll be," Anna told her with a laugh.

* * * *

After breaking their night long fast, most of the families headed outside to stand around the corral and watch. Inside the sturdy fence, wranglers bridled the horses with bits. Saving the biggest and best for the sergeant, who didn't own his own, they delivered a horse to each of the men in blue. The soldier then saddled his horse, most using the saddles the Army supplied. After outfitting the saddle with his rifle scabbard, each soldier also tied on his saddlebags and his bedroll on the back. Lifting himself into the saddle, he joined the others in the field beyond the corral to get to know the horse and how he obeyed commands.

It took much of the day, but when the horses had all been assigned, there were still soldiers who did not have one. Another day had to be spent seeking out enough horses to be purchased to outfit the remaining soldiers.

"Look at that," Eric cried as a wagon train heading west came past the coach stop while they were waiting for more horses to arrive.

Though not all the wagons were as big as the Conestogas, they all had canvas stretched over curved spines to create a roof that would protect the contents from the sun and rain.

Anna and Katrin talked briefly about asking if they could go on with that wagon train instead of waiting to travel with the Army families, but they easily decided not to.

"I'd much rather travel with our new friends, and I like the security of traveling with the soldiers," Katrin said.

Anna had to agree. The idea that they might run into threatening Indians was always at the back of their minds. "Helping Elsie and minding Eric seems to be a big help to Adam," Anna told Katrin.

"Helping in this way is the least we can do for all he's done for us. I would like to continue with them and help out."

Katrin smiled. "You don't want to leave them either, do you?"

"Well, I feel much safer here, don't you?"

Katrin smiled. "Yes, Anna, and I don't want to leave Tavis either. After we get to the fort, I'll probably never see him again. Leaving then is going to be hard, but I'd rather put it off until then."

"Staying will only make parting at Fort Abercrombie harder for both of us. Little Eric is getting very attached to me, I'm afraid. Am I doing him wrong by staying close to him when I must leave him on his own as soon as we get to the fort?"

"I think he can only be happier for having known you, Anna. And his father, too."

It was his father about whom Anna was thinking. She was much happier for knowing him and would be very sad when she had to leave him. And she knew that she had to. She and Katrin could not break the promises they had made to find the Oleson brothers and be their brides.

The families and soldiers cheered the next day at the coach stop when an assortment of hired empty wagons was lined up and ready to load. Only a few had canvas stretched over the top to protect the contents. Others were covered coaches with wooden bench seats inside and open windows and a door with another window on each side. Fabric curtains, if they worked, could be lowered over each window opening to keep out the sun or rain unless there was wind. With wind the rain would blow right in.

The last wagon to pull in was for the cook and his assistant. The tailgate folded down into a table, giving the men access to a cabinet with many drawers containing implements, bowls, and frying pans for preparing the meals on the journey. Between the cabinet and the front of the wagon was an area covered by oiled cloth where they stored the foodstuffs like beans and flour in barrels. The two men rode on the bench seat at the front and had to drive the wagon, too.

Once again the sergeant took charge of all the passengers. He assigned one or sometimes two families to each coach or wagon. The bags that could not be stored on top of the coaches in the open where they would be rained on were packed in the covered wagons to protect them. The wagon train was heading for Fort Abercrombie where they would sort out the trunks and bags when they arrived.

Not a part of any soldier's family, Anna and Katrin had to pay the wagon master at this point for being included. They had certainly expected this, but when they heard the amount, they worried about the high price. However, when they realized that all the meals for the whole trip would be included in the fare, they felt better about the price. They looked forward to having regular meals as they traveled, and they admitted they had no idea how they would have managed on their own. Along with Elsie and Eric, they were pleasantly surprised to be put in a coach with two other soldiers' wives, Alice and Rose. That meant that Jimmy, Rose's son, would be in their coach, too. He and Eric both seemed to like the idea. Alice had no children and was happy to be in a coach with other women to talk to. Both their husbands would ride their horses like the rest of the soldiers.

"I'm glad we get to travel with you, Rose," Katrin told her. "I think Eric would not like being in a coach with all adult women."

"My Jimmy is a little older than Eric, but the boys should be able to play and stay out of our hair most of the time."

"The coach looks awfully small to me. I think they'll be in our hair all the time," Katrin replied with a laugh and a shake of her head.

When the time came to get on board, the sergeant lifted each woman up to the high step with his hands at their waist. The women thanked him in turn and took their seats. Anna didn't think he did that for everyone else in the wagon train, but she knew that if there were a chance that he could be near Katrin, the sergeant would take it. She had to give him credit though. He was always available to help Elsie, too.

Katrin was the last to enter the coach. Instead of lifting her with her back to him as he had the others, she was turned to face him. His hands rested at her waist, hers on his shoulders. "Thank you, Sergeant. You are such a big help."

"Well, I sure am big," the tall man replied with a laugh, but he made no effort to move.

"Oh, but not too big. And I'm glad you are so strong."

"I like it that you don't think I'm too big."

"Oh, you're not. My sister and I are taller than most women, and I think you're just the right size for a man."

He laughed and looked up to see the other women in the coach, watching them intently. "Up you go, Miss Katrin." He lifted her with ease to the step where she released his shoulders and turned to step into the coach. Shutting the door after her, he called up to the driver, "Ready to go, Jake."

When it was his turn to get in line with the other wagons, Jake whistled to the horses and slapped the reins on their backs to get them to begin on their way. They followed other wagons onto the dirt road, allowing space between the wagons so the horses didn't have to breathe in the dust that rose from the wagon ahead of them. The stretches between towns where some grass had grown on the road helped keep the dust down. However, most of the road was just dusty packed dirt in the wagon tracks.

The positions the wagons took in the line were not always the same. The cook's wagon was most often at or near the front so he could be first in camping position and get a fire going while the other wagons circled. The others switched positions each time one pulled over off the road to give the passengers a relief stop for their personal needs.

The passengers didn't always ride inside the wagon and coaches. The horses plodded so slowly that many passengers became adept at jumping off and swinging back later on when they wanted to walk a bit for exercise or just to get off the hard seats. For some, walking was far better than bouncing around on the hard plank seats in the coaches.

Anna guessed the horses were allowed to walk at that slow pace so as not to tire them out too much. They had no replacement teams and these teams had to walk all day and every day. Apparently in no hurry, the drivers didn't seem to mind having to stop occasionally for the passengers. It gave them a break from their wooden plank seats, too.

Inside the sister's coach, the women sat in the stationary wooden bench seats in the front and back while the boys rode on the leather seat stretched in the same direction across the middle area of the coach between them. That meant each boy had a window to look out and saved them all from their arguing over the best seat by a window. And having that third seat meant the ladies could stretch their legs out under it when they wanted to.

As the day warmed and the passengers felt more uncomfortable, Alice put her head out the window and called out, "Can we stop for a few minutes, Jake?"

"Sure," he replied, and pulled the wagon out of the line. After setting the brake and securing the reins around the lever, he climbed down. Meanwhile, the young ladies and boys jumped down and disappeared into the trees beside the road to relieve themselves. When Elsie appeared at the door to get out, Jake helped her by grasping her at her waist and lifting her down from the high step. Anna saw her wince before she managed to smile and thank him. She hoped he hadn't set her down too hard. She offered her arm to Elsie for support and walked with her, but she couldn't think of a better way to lift her down without a man the size of the sergeant to cradle her in his arms.

The sergeant rode over as Katrin was returning to the coach. They talked quietly apart from the others until everyone was ready to start out again. He helped the other ladies all back into the coach, but Katrin and Alice decided they wanted to walk for a while.

"Then can we sit on your seats for a while instead of on the swinging seat?" Eric asked.

"Go right ahead," Katrin told him. "Sitting on our bags will make the wooden seat softer."

"If you don't sit on the books," Anna added with a smile.

Jake climbed to the driver's seat and turned the horses toward the road while the sergeant held up the next passing wagon so he could pull right into the line. He waved and rode back down the line of wagons.

Katrin and Alice talked as they walked beside the coach. Katrin learned that Alice had traveled all the way north to New York after the war was over, and now they were going west.

"You've seen a lot of this country, then. It's so green and beautiful."

"But I've never seen the ocean like you have coming over from Norway. I can't even imagine what it would be like to be on a boat in the middle of the ocean and not be able to see the shore in any direction. I think I would be scared," Alice said.

"We were scared," Katrin told her. "But the stories that we heard about this country made it sound so wonderful. We were also excited, as well. Like you, we are looking forward to getting a new start in the Dakota Territory." She laughed. "We just didn't know how far from New York it was."

"It's good we're traveling across the northern states. The scenery is better than going through states down south. Homes are burned out. Folks have no food to eat. If a landowner has any money the officials take it for taxes. If he has no money, instead of letting him work the land and make money to pay the taxes, they take the land and leave him and his family homeless." She shook her head slowly. "We have a chance at starting again by moving west this way."

"If we do not find the Oleson brothers we told you about, then we will have nothing like the people down south that you described. We could be homeless." Katrin looked at her. "I don't like to think of that."

Alice laughed and shook her head. "I don't think you have to worry about that. Half the men in the army company we are traveling with are unmarried. I think they would like unmarried ladies to live near the fort. In fact I don't think you would remain unmarried for long."

Katrin laughed then. "The men are nice, especially the sergeant. He works hard to make sure things go smoothly for everyone."

"He's lucky it's not a full company he has to keep track of. That would be twice as much work. The Army moved us out before they had time to enlist a full hundred in the company. I haven't counted them, but I think that we don't have much more than half that many soldiers."

"I hope it is enough to keep us safe from the Indians when we get there."

Alice nodded. "I hope so, too, but I don't think they'd let the families move out there if it wasn't pretty safe. It would be sad if a man made it through the war and was assigned out there only to die fighting the Indians." She shook her head. "But, being a soldier's wife, you gotta think of that, too."

The ladies walked in silence thinking about that sobering thought. Soon Katrin started to limp, as the back of her heels got more and more sore.

"What's wrong?" Alice asked.

"I think I'm getting blisters on the heels. These shoes aren't very good for walking. I bought them just before we left Norway, because they were sturdy and would last a long time. But the leather is still stiff."

"Here, sit down and take your shoes off."

Katrin looked at the wagon train and saw that they were ahead of their coach so she walked to the side of the road and did as Alice suggested. She was alarmed to see that her heels were both blistered and that the blisters had already broken.

The sergeant, ever vigilant, rode up. "What's wrong?" he asked, sliding from his saddle and coming to stand before her.

Katrin quickly pulled her skirt down to cover her feet, but the sergeant dropped to one knee and boldly inspected her feet anyway. He didn't remove the stockings, but he saw the wet spots on her heels from the oozing blisters.

"This is the end of your walking, Miss Katrin. And while you're in the coach, you leave your shoes off and take your stockings off, too, so your feet can heal."

"I can't go without shoes and stockings," she insisted.

"You will if you want your heels not to fester. And after a few days when they are better, you should wear two or three pairs of stockings to pad your heels if you have none that are thicker."

"But how can I…I mean I have to be able to walk from the coach when we make our stops." She felt the heat of embarrassment rise into her cheeks.

The sergeant grinned. "Don't you worry none about that, lass. I'll take care of getting you where you want to go."

"You can't do that. You have duties that keep you busy all day. You can't be watching for our coach to stop."

He laughed. "I have the time to help you, Miss Katrin. These drivers don't want to drive their horses faster than they have to, and some of these city boys were foot soldiers and never rode a horse in their life. They all like riding slow to get used to riding."

"They really don't know how to ride a horse?" Alice asked. "I never knew a man who didn't know how to ride."

The sergeant shrugged. "Even some of the country boys have only used horses to pull a plow or a small wagon. Now they're finding out that riding in a saddle all day is different. It's a lot harder on their… Well, it's harder on them," he finished with a laugh.

For the next several days, the sergeant was true to his word. When their coach made stops, the other ladies exited and then he lifted Elsie from the coach and set her down gently. Smiling at her bare feet, he lifted Katrin down last and carried her wherever she wanted to go. To give her privacy, he stepped back to the coach to chat with the others and returned to get her when he saw her begin to pick her way back barefoot.

When they stopped close by to a lake at noon for their meal, the sergeant carried Katrin to the water where she would walk into the water to soak her feet for a while. It felt good, and she never would have thought of stepping in the water barefoot if the sergeant hadn't suggested it. Being near the lake gave her a chance to wash her stained stockings, too. The passengers all longed to wash their clothes, too, but the wagon train never paused long enough to do it.

At first, Katrin was very embarrassed by the attention, so she tried to take care of her personal needs when they stopped for meals. But with the stops necessary for the other women and the boys, she got to like the attention he gave her and she got to like him more and more. Tavis was so gallant. And he knew what he was talking about when it came to blisters. After several days, she was able to put on her shoes again after slipping on extra stockings as ordered. By passing the word to other women to wear extra stockings for more padding as they walked, many avoided getting such sore heels.

At the same time, the soldiers suffered other sores that were not so easily treated. The trouble that the soldiers had riding the horses showed up first in sore leg muscles and painful backsides. For the first week or so, the men new to riding complained mostly of sore legs. Then the thick hand-sewn seams in some of their uniform trousers caused chaffing that got worse each day. The men walked more and more, leading their horses behind them, but that often didn't help, because their legs rubbed together and irritated the sores. The horses seemed to like them walking better, but the men found little relief until the cook offered bacon grease to each for their chaffed skin.

About then the soldiers discovered that the horses had their own problems with chaffing. A couple had such ill-fitting saddles that they were barely controllable. With a rider putting weight on their back, sores that had developed became so painful that the horses would try to rid themselves of the riders. The problems were all finally sorted out and the sores treated.

Lacking any ability of riding bareback, a few soldiers had to stop riding their horses altogether. Some of those men showed no signs of remorse and instead rode happily on the drivers' seats next to the driver hired with the wagon. The soldiers' horses were tied to the back of a wagon until they could get saddles that fit.

* * * *

The dirt road that the wagon train followed most of the time passed through several small towns as they rode west. When they passed one late enough in the day, the wagon train would stop for the night near the town. They rode through the town so the passengers got to see what was there, and then the drivers circled the wagons beyond the buildings for the night. While the drivers and soldiers took care of the horses, the women were sometimes able to walk into town before it got too dark.

The cooks took advantage of being able to shop for what they needed in the mercantile when there was one, though many towns were too small to have a business of any kind. They were spots on the route where people had built their homes close together for company and for protection. Once their horses were corralled for the night, the soldiers who had no families often headed for the saloon. Once in a while a family who could afford it dined at the restaurant if there was one.

Anna and Katrin imagined that this was what the Dakota Territory would be like. There would be nearby stores at which they could buy what they needed. Thinking that, they wondered what the American stores were like. Now that Katrin's heels were healed, they decided to walk to town one late afternoon to see what the mercantile had to offer. Not seeing any other women going that way, they headed out alone.

As they walked past the first two buildings, they saw their first Indian, actually two of them. They were sitting on the ground, leaning against the end of the building that held the saloon. One seemed to be asleep and the other held out his hand as they passed. He grunted something unintelligible. With long dirty hair covering much of their faces, and wrapped in dirty blankets, they didn't look as frightening as the sisters had expected. Seeing them only added to their confusion about why the soldiers were talking about needing to kill them. The sisters quickened their steps to get beyond them.

"They must be Indians, but they don't look very frightening," Anna whispered to her sister as they walked on.

"No, they didn't look like they could hurt anyone."

"It doesn't look like the Army would have a hard time moving them out of the area, but no one in town seems to mind them sitting there."

"They're begging and no one is helping them either," Katrin noted with a glance back.

They continued moving quickly to get past the Indians and didn't notice that they were passing in front of the open entrance to the saloon. Seeing them coming, two men came out the swinging door and stepped in front of them to stop them.

"Well, look what we have here," one said in slurred words.

The sisters understood what he had said, but they were not about to respond. They linked arms and turned to step around them without comment.

"Now, don't rush off so fast," the other said. "We ain't seen two beauties like you with golden hair in this town before." He stepped around in front of the ladies again, just about tripping over his own feet in the process. With one man ahead of them and one behind them, the sisters couldn't move.

"Come on inside and let us buy you a drink," the first managed.

"The ladies don't want a drink," a firm but familiar voice from behind them said.

Releasing the breath they had been holding, the sisters quickly sidestepped toward the dirt street where the sergeant and the private, who was most often with him, sat on their horses.

"Cain't do that, soldier. The war's over and we saw 'em first," one of the men from the saloon insisted. "And we don't need no help."

The sergeant slid from his saddle to the ground. He handed his reins to the private and stepped toward the two men, towering over them. "You want to go back into the saloon on your feet or do you want to stay here out cold on your backs in the street?"

The drunken pair looked up at the big man standing with his hands on his hips and quickly made their way back into the saloon. They all heard hoots from other men inside who had witnessed their cowardly behavior.

The sergeant turned to the sisters. He laid a hand on the back of each of the waists and urged them to walk away from the front of the saloon. "Ladies, this is not a safe place for you to be."

"We wanted to see what they have in the mercantile," Katrin said, stopping but pointing to the store just beyond where they stood.

"We have never seen the inside of a store in America," Anna added.

A broad grin brightened his face. "Well, we have just enough time before we must get back to the wagons for supper. Allow me, ladies." He held out a bent arm on each side for the ladies to take hold of. "Private, bring the horses," he ordered over his shoulder.

"Yes, sir," the young man said. He spurred them on to the store where he tied them to the hitching post out front. When the sergeant and the sisters got to the door, he followed them inside.

It didn't take them long to tour the small store. "They even have a wood burning cook stove and a table and chairs. They have almost anything you could want to fill a house," Katrin concluded.

"As long as you can pay for it," the sergeant put in with a chuckle. "But I think the stove is what keeps the store warm in the winter and I'd bet many a checkers game gets played on that table when the snow has covered the ground."

Katrin couldn't help but ask, "How would a family buy goods to start out if they didn't have any money? How will poor families like

Alice's make out? The war left them with nothing much beyond the clothes on their backs."

"It won't be easy. The government is giving out the land free, but to make a home on it would be near to impossible if you can't make what you need yourself," the sergeant told her.

"If you can't make it and if you have nothing?"

"I saw a lot of people down south had to make do with what they could find. And folks helped each other. I expect it's like that out west, too," the sergeant told them.

"Then, I think we are lucky. We have men waiting for us who have already built a home. We don't need to worry about what we would do if we had to make it on our own with our limited funds."

The sergeant frowned and said no more. They circled through the store toward the front door. Katrin saw large brown bars of soap on the counter.

"We will need to buy soap to clean our clothes with when we get there," she commented. "The one bar we brought is almost gone."

"Ya don't want to run out of soap," the private said. "My maw made me take some in my pack when I left to join the patrol, in case I got a hankering to take a bath."

Katrin laughed. The private had been standing by them so silently that his voice had startled her. "You mother is smart. It's something we didn't even think of needing more than one. We should have brought more."

Finished circling the store, the private held the front door for her and Anna as they walked out onto the street. He untied the reins for both horses, and they all began to walk toward the wagon train campsite, well away from the buildings so they would not pass close to the saloon door again.

"Shouldn't we wait for the sergeant?" Katrin asked, looking back into the store to see that he was at the counter talking with the storeowner.

He joined them a few moments later with a grin on his face and two small packages wrapped in brown paper in his hand. He fell into step next to Katrin and gave one package to her and the other to Anna as they walked. "There, now you each have a big bar of some good soap," he said.

Katrin looked at the package and then up at the tall man walking beside her. "You bought us soap?"

He nodded, still grinning.

"That is very kind of you," Anna put in. "But we cannot accept a gift from you, Sergeant. Where we come from, that is not proper."

"Oh, but it's not a gift," he insisted.

Anna frowned and glanced at Katrin and then met his gaze again. "Well, what is it then?"

"It's just one person heading west who is helping another. Just like we talked about. Out here folks help each other."

"But..." Anna began, but she didn't know what to say.

"Thank you, Tavis," Katrin said softly with a smile for the good man. "That was very kind of you to...to help us." All four of them laughed.

The walk back to the campsite with the soldiers was pleasant, and no one gave them a moment's trouble when they passed the saloon. Katrin forgot about the groom waiting for her in the Dakota Territory as she walked with one hand tucked in the sergeant's bent arm and her other hand holding the precious bar of soap that he had given her.

* * * *

To this point traveling beyond St. Paul had been pleasant with the weather cooperating. The days were not too hot and the nights were cool enough that the coach didn't seem too stuffy for sleeping. There was the annoying problem of the mosquitoes that were larger and more persistent than others they had experienced. They were bad during the day, but they were thicker and more annoying at night. Eric was particularly miserable and had bites all over his face and arms where his skin was exposed. They even seemed to be large enough to bite right through his shirt.

"Please try not to itch them," Elsie told him. "You're making them bleed and I don't want them to get sore."

"But I can't stop. They itch too much," he protested, scratching one as he spoke.

"You haven't seen mosquitoes until you've trudged through a swamp down south in the summer. The only thing we used to have to stop the itch was mud," Rose told them. "We mixed soil with a little water and put a dab on the bites. It would dry there and seemed to help."

Eric and Jimmy were anxious to try it. The next time they stopped for the noon meal near a lake, they walked to the shore. With the women watching out for their safety, the boys stepped barefoot into the water a foot or two until they were in it ankle deep. Their toes dug into the muddy bottom. Leaning down they scooped up handfuls of mud and turned back to the women for help. Dipping in their fingers, the women placed the brown mud on the swollen bites on the boy's exposed skin. They even dabbed each other in a few places that itched a great deal.

"Now don't touch the mud. It has to dry to draw out the swelling," Rose instructed them.

Returning to the wagon train, the boys enjoyed telling everyone who would listen exactly why they had brown spots on their skin. Soon all the children and many of the adults were covered with mud spots, but the bites were all still itchy.

"At least they aren't scratching while they wait for the mud to dry," Elsie said with a smile. "And with that much mud on their faces and necks, I don't think the mosquitoes can bite through it."

By that evening the mud was gone from their skin, not because they scratched it off, but because the good weather they had been enjoying didn't last. Passing between two of the many lakes that dotted the region between St. Paul and the Dakota Territory, they rode into a heavy rain that showed no signs of letting up the next day. The rain came down so hard that it got rid of the mosquitoes flying around, but it left huge rain puddles in the ruts in the road and softened the tracks. The puddles were often deep, and the wet mud was slick and dangerous. The horses' hooves sometimes sank into the soil and made strange sucking sounds with each step. They were forced into an even slower walk. The drivers let them take the slower pace so they wouldn't get injured.

With the rain falling, no one wanted to stop for anything, but a few times a day, the coaches couldn't avoid it. There was room in the covered wagons to have a temporary chamber pot for the riders, but not in the coaches. There was no room and no privacy. They had to stop.

In low lying areas and closer to the lakeshores they passed, the ground was saturated off the road and even swampy, but the drivers couldn't tell that in the hard rain. If the wagons left the worn path on the road to make a stop for the passengers, the wheels often got mired in the mud. Returning to the coach after a quick visit to the trees, the coach passengers sometimes stepped through ankle-deep mud to climb in. As other coaches and wagons passed, the driver cracked the whip over the horses and shouted at them to get the stopped wagons moving again. With the horses' hooves also buried in the mud as deep as the wheels were, they couldn't move the coach.

“You have to get out. I can’t get it moving with so much weight in it,” the driver shouted to the passengers.

“Get out in the rain again?”

“If you want me to move into position in the wagon train you do.”

While the passengers climbed out again, the driver whistled to the soldiers to help him. With their horses on each side of the team, they grasped the bridles. When the coach was empty, the driver tried again to get the coach moving. With less weight to pull, they finally managed. Pulling back on the packed road, the driver stopped the coach and held up the rest of the train while he waited until the passengers got inside again. Wet, muddy, and cold, they huddled together inside to share body heat and try to get warm and dry again. All the while they complained that they should have gotten to ride in the covered wagons, too.

Oblivious to the muddy mess now inside the coach on the floor, on their shoes, and on the women’s skirts, Eric loved the excitement and seeing all the men working so hard to keep the wagon train moving. Thinking of ways to play in the rain, he and Jimmy hung their heads out of the curtained window in the rain and stuck their tongues out to catch the drops. They watched another coach mired in the mud as they passed. “I wish we would get stuck again, too. Wouldn’t that be fun to get out in the mud again?”

No one in the coach agreed with him except Jimmy.

Chapter 6

Anna leaned against the tree in hopes that the leaves and branches above her would shield her from the rain. It did seem to help as long as she stayed on the downwind side of the big tree. She thought she was being foolish, but she couldn't get back into the coach just yet. Everyone had ridden in the coach with no chance to get a break walking, because of the constant rain.

She frowned and looked from wagon to wagon in the circle around the one fire the men had managed to get going. The cook had tried to heat the beans in the fire for supper, but they ended up not getting very warm.

Thinking back to rain storms in Norway, she remembered her mother making cups of hot milk with a little butter and sugar in them. The warm liquid going down their throats warmed up their whole bodies. "I wish I had a cup now," she murmured to herself.

A horse approached her protected spot, and she looked up to see Adam, rain dripping off the brim of his hat, but a smile on his handsome face.

"If you're standing there waiting for a train, I don't think one is coming this way—not yet anyway. Give it a few years."

She laughed as he slid down from his horse and took a position next to her, leaning against the trunk of the tree with their shoulders pressed against each other.

"Do you really think they will build rails all the way out here?"

"I imagine that they will build them all the way to the west coast."

"That will be a wonder."

"Now that the war is over, men can put their minds to doing other things," he offered.

She looked up at him and smiled. "I don't know how you managed to have them finish the rails to St. Paul from Chicago, but I'm glad you did."

Though it was getting dark, she could see that he was grinning. "I wish I could take credit for that," he said.

"Well, what else can you do? Can you stop the rain? I really think we've had enough. I don't think I've dried off for days. And at the slow rate that we are traveling, I think we are going to take forever to get to the fort."

"Not quite forever." A deep laugh rumbled in his chest.

She liked the sound of his laughter. A gust of wind shook the leaves above them so that the rain sitting on them fell. Anna wiped her face with the sleeve of her coat and groaned. "It doesn't do any good to wipe off the rain with a wet sleeve."

"You're not cold are you? I don't want you to get sick."

"I put my coat on to go out and then take it off and hang it over the window in the coach to dry a little before I need it again. It doesn't keep me dry, but it's better than nothing."

"Would it help if I put my arm around you?" he asked, putting his arm around her shoulder before she could answer. With their faces close together, his hat kept the rain off her face, too.

"That is better, but we shouldn't stand here like this."

"It's so dark now that I don't think anyone can see us," he replied.

"I should go. I don't want them to worry."

"Just a few minutes more," he insisted.

She nodded and wanted to lean her forehead against his cheek. Instead she looked at the coach and saw Rose climbing in with Jimmy and Eric.

"I worry about Elsie getting sick in this weather," Adam said.

"I can hear some of the others coughing, but no one in our coach is."

"Good. Take care of yourself." He grinned. "Hmm. I think that means no more standing under trees in a rain storm." They heard thunder in the distance as the sky was brightened with a lightning strike. "Hey, that's getting closer. Back to the coach with you."

"Yes, sir," she said, laughing, and turned in his arm to face him. She raised her arm for a mock salute.

Before she realized what he was going to do, he kissed her lightly on her lips. Their gazes locked for a moment, and then he turned her toward her coach and gave her a little shove.

"Good night," she said without turning back as she ran to the coach. She couldn't see him, because it was so dark out, but she heard the squeak of wet leather as he mounted his horse and rode on around the outside of the circle of wagons.

"You take care, too," she whispered before opening the coach door and climbing in.

She fell asleep quite quickly that night not feeling cold at all since his kiss.

When she opened the coach door the next morning, it was to see the sun rising into a blue sky. No evidence of rain clouds could be found. Wet coats, quilts and blankets, and even some clothes decorated the wagon sides as they left the camp spot after breaking their fast.

* * * *

The second time the wagon train passengers saw Indians, the circumstances were very different from seeing one asleep next to one begging in a town days before. The wagon train had just passed through a small town where few people could be seen. Even the saloon was quiet and appeared empty. If the travelers saw anyone on the street when they entered the town, the individuals walked rapidly and disappeared into one of the buildings without so much as a wave in the wagon train's direction. Doors were shut and the windows shuttered or curtained. While the wagons and soldiers passed through town, no one came outside to watch or talk to them.

Used to people coming out to wave and join in brief conversations as they moved through, the soldiers were on alert. Something appeared to be very wrong. Not certain what it was, the lieutenant ordered his men to ride in single file alongside the wagons instead of having half in front and the other half bringing up the rear as they had been doing.

"This is like a ghost town," Rose said, looking out the coach window. "'Cepting them buildings don't look old and worn down."

"I wonder where everyone went," Anna replied. "It makes me feel nervous that no one is on the street."

The women watched out the windows on both sides of the coach.

"Do you smell smoke?" Katrin asked.

Rose nodded. "Yeah. It's getting stronger. It must be up ahead of us."

The women looked out the coach windows on both sides searching for the source of the smell as well as for people. Anna leaned her head out the window a little so she could see beside the road ahead of them.

"I can see a gray cloud of smoke rising slowly above the wagons at the head of the line," she said. "We're heading right to whatever is burning."

Eric and Jimmy stuck their heads out the window in the door to see for themselves. "I can't see what is burning," Eric complained.

They heard the lieutenant shout orders that sent several of the soldiers on ahead to see what it was.

"Maybe everyone from town is out fighting the fire," Anna suggested. "That would explain the empty town."

The soldiers sent to investigate galloped back to the wagon train in just a few minutes and reported to the lieutenant, but in voices that they could not hear back in the coach. All at once he shouted at the coach drivers to speed up. Other soldiers passed the order down the line of wagons as they rode to the rear. Whips cracked and drivers shouted and whistled as they all urged the horses to an unusually fast pace.

"Why are we going so fast? I want to see the fire," Jimmy said, his head out the window to see what was going on.

"Oh, dear, I hope it's not a prairie fire," Elsie said, clutching the frame of the side of the coach to stabilize herself during the faster and rougher ride. "Eric, you'd better get back inside the window. I don't know how sturdy the latch is on that door. I don't want you falling out."

"I wish we knew if we are going faster to keep us from some danger to the wagon train," Alice put in.

"This pace can't be fast enough to keep us from at least seeing what is on fire," Alice guessed.

"I don't think we need to worry that it's a danger to us. There's not enough smoke for it to be a prairie fire," Anna said to comfort Elsie.

"That's good," Elsie replied. "And I hope we don't have to ride this fast for very long."

Then Anna saw the reason for their speed. "I can see it. A small house has burned to the ground. Oh, and a nearby barn big enough to hold several horses burned, too."

"Only some of the rocks stacked together for the fireplace and chimney are still on top of each other," Rose added from her vantage point of the back seat window. "Smoke is still rising, because the fire is still smoldering, but the structure's collapsed."

Looking beyond the blackened scene, Anna suddenly gasped. She jerked the coach window curtain free from the tieback and pulled it down to cover her window and the window in the door where the boys had been looking out.

"Wait, I want to see out," Eric told her as he tried to lift the curtain again.

"No," she said. "You don't need to see this."

Anna looked at Rose and tipped her head toward the complaining boys. Then she shook her head, but she didn't say anything more. Rose and Anna closed the windows next to her seats.

"You boys can go back to playing with your stick soldiers. You don't need to see every single thing that we pass," Rose told them.

"And the closed curtain may keep out some of that awful smelling smoke," Alice put in.

Anna mouthed the words thank you.

"Aw, let us see," Jimmy insisted as he reached past Eric to try to open the curtain again.

"No," Anna said, holding the curtain down. She had to clear her throat to make her voice strong again. "Please, go back to your game."

"Jimmy, sit down with Eric and stop this," Rose told her son in no uncertain terms. "None of us needs to see what is out there."

The other women all looked at Anna, but no one asked what it was. Anna just gave her head a little shake. There would be plenty of time to learn the details later when the small boys could not hear.

However, closing out the scene for the others did not erase it from Anna's memory. She could still picture the five Indians hung by their necks from trees beyond where the barn had been. She had seen that their bodies were bloody, too. Had they been shot and maybe beaten before they were hung or after? She shuddered at the thought.

The passengers hung on to their seats for stability as the coach sped along with all the wagons to a level rise within sight of a lake about a mile beyond the scene of the hanging. There they all pulled off the road and circled as they did each evening. The ground was firm enough there and the drivers had no trouble.

Despite the early hour, the lieutenant told everyone they would be stopping there for the night. He also ordered that all non-Army passengers stay at the campsite and not go back down the road.

The women and children went about the chores to get ready for the night while the cooks started a fire to fix supper. The lieutenant took about half of the men and rode back toward town. Several carried shovels and each of them had checked to be certain their rifles were loaded and ready to shoot. The sergeant and the soldiers remaining at the campsite watched for trouble that might threaten the families. The sergeant came over to the coach as soon as he could to help Elsie down.

"Are they going off to fight with shovels?" Eric asked him after watching the other soldiers leave.

He looked up at Katrin who shook her head and shrugged. She didn't know what to say.

"Nah," the sergeant said. "They're just going to throw more dirt on the fire to be sure it's out. We sure don't want a prairie fire to start out here."

"Oh, I didn't think of that," Eric said. "That's a good idea."

But putting out the last remnants of the fire was not all the men did. When the smoldering fires were covered with dirt and not in any danger of spreading, the lieutenant ordered them to cut down the hanging bodies.

"They were all dead when somebody hung them, Lieutenant," one of the men said who was cutting the ropes. "I seen enough bodies down south to know. Why'd they hang 'em up here where everyone would see them when they was already shot dead?"

"Probably just for that reason—to let everyone who passed see them," he replied. "Maybe it's a warning to other Indians not to come here."

"I heard the man running the coach stop say that bands of Indians were hitting white folks' places to the west. But at the saloon where we stopped a few nights ago, they said the raids were northwest of here, but not this close. I guess the Indians don't get much resistance from the farm folk around here so they keep on raiding."

"Well, these folks sure hit back," another soldier put in.

"And that's why we're heading west—so we can get them murderers out of the territory," yet another said.

"But I wonder where the folks who lived here are. I don't see nobody around," a soldier looking around the remains of the barn said.

The taller soldier pointed toward a spot several yards farther from the road. "I'd say that's where they are now."

Four grave mounds covered with stones to keep out animals were lined up between the tree and the remains of a split rail fence beyond. Two were long enough for adults and two were much shorter as might be needed for children.

"Damn, I seen enough of burned out homes with graves in the front yard when I was fighting down south."

"We all have," the other soldier said.

"I didn't expect to see that here before we even get to the Territory."

"Lieutenant, it looks like help came from town in time to shoot the Indians, but not fast enough to save the family," a taller soldier guessed.

"They buried the farm folk at least."

"Then they strung up them Indians and run back to town and barricaded themselves in their houses. They made it look like nobody was there, but I could see people peeking out through the curtains or looking down from the roof."

"They don't want to be taken by surprise again."

"I wouldn't either," the Lieutenant told them. "Let's get these bodies buried."

The soldiers dragged the Indians' bodies to the field beyond the house and barn. With all the men working, they dug a wide enough hole in short order and buried the Indians.

When they were done with the grave, the lieutenant ordered his men to mount up, but he held his arm up to hold them there. "Before we go back, let's agree to keep these details to ourselves. No sense scaring the women and children, but this means we have to be on the lookout day and night from now on. If these Indians have friends out there who are planning to get even with whites, we may have our hands full. And traveling with all our families, that's the last thing we want."

Several comments showed his men agreed. He waved his arm over his head to direct them to follow him back to where the wagons had stopped for the night.

After supper that night, the lieutenant told everyone that they would be starting out at first light each day from now on and not stopping until near dark. "The farther west we get, the more watchful we have to be. If you have room, the women and children should sleep in the wagons and coaches at night instead of on the ground under it."

Murmurs of protest rose immediately. To sleep in the coaches meant that some people had to sleep sitting up. The two Army wives in the coach with Anna and Katrin had been leaving most nights to sleep with their husbands out under the stars. Now they would be staying in the coach, too.

"I know it's hard, but...well, just do it. And you men sleep with your rifles. Make sure your arms are loaded."

Several "yes, sirs" were heard as the families went to their wagons to follow orders despite the discomfort they would cause.

The lieutenant headed for Eric to be sure he was bedded down safely in the coach. After a few minutes together, Eric climbed into the coach.

Anna had just returned to the coach when Adam headed down the line of wagons. "Lieutenant," she called just loud enough for him to hear as she quickened her step to catch up with him.

Adam turned and smiled when he saw her. He stopped and waited for her to catch up. Taking her arm, he walked away from the circle of wagons for several yards where their conversation wouldn't be overheard.

"I...I saw what was back there beyond the burned farm," Anna began.

Adam frowned, his eyes opening wider with alarm. "Did..."

She shook her head. "I pulled the curtains in the coach down as fast as I could so Eric and the others did not see them."

The lieutenant blew out the breath he'd been holding. "Thank you for that. I wouldn't want to have to explain to him what happened out there."

"Was that all of them? Did they kill them all? Or are there more out there that we have to worry about? Is that why we're putting in more time traveling each day?"

"I don't know if there are more around here," he said shaking his head. "I don't know how to tell where they are."

"But you think they might be around here. And that's why you told your soldiers to sleep with their rifles."

Stepping closer, he took a gentle hold of her shoulders. "We're all going to do our best to not let anything happen to you or any of our families. But, the Army brought us out here to clear the area of Indians and they are fighting back. They are out here, and we don't know where."

"I'm frightened."

He tugged her against his chest and wrapped his arms around her. She went willingly and wrapped her arms around his waist. "Being frightened isn't bad. It will keep you alert and observant."

She nodded, her cheek rubbing against the rough wool of his jacket. He smelled of the outdoors and honest sweat.

"I…I can't be near Eric every minute to protect him. I am very grateful that you watch him and see that he stays close to you and his grandmother."

Anna leaned back a little, but didn't drop her arms from his waist. The cool night air replaced the warmth of his embrace. "You have done so much for us that I will always be grateful. Watching Eric is the least I can do for you. He's a good boy and no trouble at all."

"Thank you," he said. The campfire light reaching them between the trees reflected in his eyes as he bent closer and kissed her on the cheek.

She smiled and closed her eyes for a moment. She wished he had kissed her lips and she had no right to wish that. Stepping back farther so that she had to drop her arms from around him, he offered his bent arm for her hand for the short walk back to their coach. She grasped it with both her hands and walked slowly beside him back to her coach. He touched the brim of his hat and walked on.

As Anna climbed into the coach, she could see that all the other women and the boys were inside, ready to retire. They had already decided Elsie and the two boys would sleep lying on the wooden seats in the coach. With their heads at opposite ends, the boys kicked at each other a bit, but being tired, they soon fell asleep.

The Army wives and Katrin and Anna lay on the floor. Even sleeping on their folded blankets with their rolled up coats as pillows wasn't very comfortable. So starting out at first light didn't turn out to be much of a hardship. Getting up was preferred over staying on the hard bed in the stuffy coach.

Anna found sleeping nearly impossible, and she didn't feel like herself the next day. What she had seen at the burned out farmstead was more horrendous than anything she had ever witnessed in her life. Seeing the bloody scene before she could close the curtain had changed her. In all her years, she'd never imagined such a scene, and couldn't help but think of the letter Ingor had sent to his uncle from the Dakota Territory. He said the Indians had saved his life his first winter there, when he got lost in a blizzard that he hadn't seen coming.

Now, Anna could not reconcile that caring action toward a white man with the murdering devastation she had witnessed the day before. Everyone assumed the Indians had raided and burned the farm. She didn't know what drove them to doing that, but their actions would certainly be the motivation for killing them.

Deciding to walk alongside the coach in the cooler morning air when the wagon train moved out, she often looked around, searching for Indians hiding behind trees or in the high grass. Was this what her life was going to be like in the Dakota Territory? Always on the lookout for Indians who would harm her? Always feeling afraid of what might happen each day or the next? She didn't like the idea.

After a night spent in the stuffy coach, Anna encouraged Eric and Jimmy to walk with her, too. She didn't shy away when they brought her a frog to examine or when they chased a rabbit that got away.

The lieutenant rode over to their coach to check on his son and mother-in-law several times each day. Anna looked forward to talking with him as they walked together after his visit with them.

Eric jumped at the chance to sit on his horse as they walked, but he quickly wanted to return to play with Jimmy if the horse wasn't going to go any faster.

"I see Elsie is in the coach each time I ride over here. Does she walk at all?" he asked.

Anna shook her head. "She doesn't seem to have the energy. Even when she must get out, we have to help her. I know the bumpy ride is painful on her joints, but she is able to sleep during the day when the coach is moving and that's good."

"I wish I knew how to make it easier for her."

"There's nothing more you could do."

"I didn't think she should come, but she has no family left. My wife was her only child and her own husband passed years ago."

"She loves being with Eric and he loves her. She tells him stories about when his mother was a little girl about his age."

"Good. I don't want him to forget her even though he never knew her."

Anna nodded, but added nothing more.

He met her gaze and said, "Thank you."

Anna shook her head. "You don't need to keep saying that. I can see that to survive out here, we must all give help to anyone who needs it."

She laid her hand on his sleeve and gave him a reassuring squeeze. She felt the warm strength of his arm and knew she could always count on him to protect them all. She should keep her distance and not depend on him as she did, but she welcomed having his strength to see her through the trip. She would be lost without him. What would happen when she had to leave him? She couldn't let herself think about that now.

"Life in the west isn't easy. We all know the Army has been assigned there to keep the peace."

She nodded. "I understand that, but it is not what we expected. In Norway they painted a picture of this country as a land of great opportunity with acres and acres of free land and a safe way of life."

"It will be safe for you and your family soon. The Army is going to clear the way for more immigrants as fast as they can. That's why they are moving us west. And more settlers are coming every year. We wouldn't be bringing our families with us if it wasn't going to be safe." He smiled.

Anna looked at his smile and wanted to believe him. "I hope so."

"And don't you worry. I'll help you find the brothers you seek."

"Oh, yes, of course," she replied, feeling both happy and sad at the news. "It would be good to have help to find them. I don't know how to even begin."

"When we get to the fort, people may know of them there. They will tell us where to find them living. There aren't very many people in the territory yet. I think someone will know where they are."

She nodded but said nothing in response as she felt a lump growing in her throat. She swallowed hard but couldn't say that she was afraid that they would find them. No, she couldn't say that a part of her didn't want to find them at all. She had promised to marry one of them and now, walking on a wagon trail with Adam, she wondered how she could have ever promised such a thing without even knowing them.

He stopped walking and moved his horse to stand between them and the wagon train moving slowly by them several yards away.

"I know it's not something you like to think about, but you must consider what you will do if we don't find them. They might have met with an accident, or they might have moved on west along the Oregon Trail. You didn't hear about where they were living before you left Norway?"

"No. Ingor sent a letter to his uncle to tell his brother to come join him. Lars sent just one to say that he had arrived in Philadelphia and was leaving to find Ingor. After that no letters arrived." She met his gaze and noted the frown on his face. "I hadn't thought that something might have happened to them. We would never know then, would we?"

"Anna, I want you to promise me something." He pulled off a glove and held it in the hand that gripped the reins. He took her hand in his bare one and they stopped walking. "Promise me that if it doesn't work out for you, with one of the brothers, I mean, you will come find me. I'll keep you safe. I promise."

Lifting her chin with his gloveless fingers, he kissed her then on the lips. It ended nearly as soon as it began. "Promise?" He waited for her tearful nod and then swung into his saddle. Once his glove was replaced, he spurred his horse on.

Anna swiped away her tears with her fingertips, hoping no one passing in a wagon could see them. She had liked his kiss and that was wrong. Very wrong. She was beginning to care too much for a man who was not to be her husband.

Chapter 7

The signal from the soldiers riding in front of the wagon train brought all the wagons and coaches to a stop. Jake, the driver of the sisters' coach, knew what it was without being told. He'd driven this route before. He tied the reins to the brake lever once it was set and jumped down from his high perch. "There's water ahead," he told the women in the coach. "We got a river to cross." The passengers of all the wagons got out to stretch their legs and wait for directions.

The lieutenant, the sergeant, and several soldiers and the drivers gathered beside the river.

"I didn't think she'd be this high now," one of the drivers said.

"All that rain must have fallen upstream, too. It filled her up," another replied.

"Can we get the wagons and horses across?" the lieutenant asked. "Safely?"

"We can't promise nothing, but let us look around. We gotta see what the flooding did to her this spring. If we find a good crossing place with firm banks that aren't too steep, we should be able to," the cook said.

The lieutenant nodded his approval to the drivers. They split into two groups. One walked upstream and one down. "Sergeant, pass the word to tie everything down on the wagons. If the bottom of this river is rocky or not level, we don't want anything falling off. It will be gone downstream before we could get it in this current."

The sergeant saluted before he and several soldiers rode back along the wagons and coaches. They gave the order and stopped often to help the families tie down their goods. The drivers of the covered wagons recommended taking down the canvas tops.

"If we tip over in the fast water, the canvas will act like a sail and take the wagon downstream fast until it hits something or sinks."

No one liked the sounds of that, so the job of removing the canvas was assigned to several soldiers. As the wagons were prepared, they lined up for the crossing. With soldiers in the river on their horses, the water hit their heels and made the horses nervous. Not wanting any of the women and children in danger, the soldiers lifted them onto their saddles ahead of themselves and rode them across while their wagon was driven across with only the driver aboard. The children loved the adventure, but few escaped without wet feet and splashed clothing.

The low-slung wagons with the smaller wheels seemed to float on the water at the deepest area. The problem came when the flowing water turned them in the river and pulled at the horses to turn. But before the soldiers could move in and help, the wheels caught in the muddy bottom. The horses pulled the wagon and the wheels slid in the mud to straighten it. The horses' hooves sank into the muddy river bottom, but the mud allowed the wagon wheels to even move sideways with no damage.

One of the smaller covered wagons had the smaller sized wheels that had been put on to replace larger ones that weren't available. When the current in the river lifted it and turned it, the horses panicked. Several soldiers rode into the water to hold their reins and keep them in line, but the unevenly loaded wagon began to list to one side. The soldiers got the team to the shallower water and finally the wagon wheels hit bottom. But as the horses pulled it toward the shore, one wheel hit a rough outcropping and broke. The metal rim was hanging from the axle and several spokes and part of the wheel were missing. The driver got the team up the bank and not much farther. The broken wheel caught in the mud and dug in.

"What do you need to repair it?" the sergeant asked as he rode up to see what the problem was.

"A wheelwright!" the driver shouted as he tied the reins to the brake handle and climbed down.

"Unless you want to walk a long ways, you'd better come up with a better idea."

"Yes, yes. I have a spare on the freight wagon that should work."

The sergeant ordered a few soldiers who had already crossed to help the drivers. They had to lift the wagon and put logs and rock under it to get it high enough to change the wheel. By the time they got the wagon raised and secure, the freight wagon had crossed. The other drivers helped untie the spare wheel and put it on after removing the broken one. The pieces of the broken one were packed in the freight wagon. Nothing was thrown away that might have parts that could be used again. The family that had been riding in the wagon could only find a place in the shade to sit and wait.

The crossing was not a quick job and the rest of the day was taken crossing the river and replacing the broken wheel. The wagon train camped for the night just beyond the river. Once the mud settled in the water after the crossing, the soldiers filled the water barrels lashed to the sides of the wagons.

Thankful that everyone had gotten across safely, the families and soldiers gathered for dinner in a light happy mood. The lieutenant thanked everyone for the hard work and cooperation in the crossing. He also reminded them to be watchful as they moved on first thing in the morning.

* * * *

In addition to the food that the cook bought at a mercantile as they traveled, the soldiers helped fill the larder, too. The lieutenant sent ahead hunting parties to bag what they could. Two particularly eager privates, Enid and Alfred, always volunteered. They had joined the company at New York, but had come from a Confederate unit in the Virginia hills where they had lived like Jethro and Rose. They had signed up to go to the Dakota Territory because they had nothing left back home either. Their families had lost what land they had, and there was nothing left to scratch out a living on.

"We headed for the open spaces up north with our hearts set on getting a new start," Enid explained when the sergeant had questioned them initially. It was a common reason many had for signing up.

"We got no money, no place to go home to. Heading out to Dakota Territory where we got a chance at a good life seems like the thing to do," Alfred told him.

"You got that right," Enid agreed with a tap of his fist to Alfred's shoulder.

They signed the Army papers with their X and that was that. The war was over and two more confederate soldiers had joined the Union Army.

Their life in the Army was not always a smooth one. As the company moved west, if there ever were a disagreement among the soldiers, it would most likely involve this pair. The clothes on their backs were all they owned. When they joined up there had been no blue uniforms available to give them to wear as with some of the others such as Jethro. However, these two wore what they had and were sensitive if anyone commented on their gray confederate trousers with an ill-fitting blue Yankee jacket and a blue uniform hat.

Early on in the train from New York City, Katrin had asked the sergeant where they got a Yankee jacket when the Army didn't have any more with which to outfit their men.

"You don't want to know," he'd insisted.

She understood then, that he figured the pair got them off of dead Union soldiers. She shivered at the thought and the sergeant had been kind enough to quickly move on to talk about other things. She understood though that having nothing could lead one to desperate measures. It brought to mind how little money she and her sister had. What would happen to them and how would they survive if they could not find the Oleson brothers?

Hunting seemed to be the misfit pair's forte and no one complained about what they brought back for supper. The meals ranged from possum or rabbit stew to venison steaks and stew. They often found wild onions, too, that the cook added in. A few such successful hunting trips and Enid and Alfred earned the respect of the soldiers and the passengers on the wagon train. After that comments about their uniforms were rare.

What the pair couldn't come up with for dinner, the cook often found at farms that they passed near. It was a nice treat when he could find a smoker in operation. They could smell it from a long ways off and three or four soldiers including Enid and Alfred would ride over. The cook would go, too, and the farmers running the smoker always seemed happy to sell a slab of bacon or a cured ham. They weren't as salty or as firm as the men from Virginia remembered from back home, but they sure were good.

If the farmwife had loaves of bread to sell, a lunch of a slice of ham between two pieces of bread meant they didn't have to stop for longer than to put it together. The families and soldiers could eat that at noon while they walked or rode. Sometimes the wagon train passed close enough to a dairy herd for the children to get a drink of fresh milk. That was a treat when their everyday fare was water or watered down coffee.

The cook knew that they couldn't count on making a fire on rainy days. Keeping a supply of cooked bacon strips and baking double the number biscuits when he had a fire meant he always had food to serve. He only had a problem if the rain lasted more than a day. Then the pot of beans that he simmered each day came in handy.

* * * *

Katrin admired the sergeant. It was his job to see that the wagon train and the soldiers moved smoothly in their day-to-day routines and he managed to do that everyday. She could see that the men respected him. Many had fought along side of Lieutenant Johnson and the sergeant in the war. When the lieutenant was ordered to go west with this company, men wanted to stay with him. Though they knew nothing about manning the fort or fighting Indians, they volunteered to stay together for duty in Dakota Territory.

"When we told the lieutenant we all wanted to go west with him, he couldn't believe it at first," Tavis told Katrin with a laugh. "Most of us are Eastern boys and he never expected that. But I think we all wanted to go where the air smelled fresh and a man could get a piece of land he could call his own when his time in the Army ended."

"Will there be any land left when we get there?" Katrin asked on one of their daily walks together beside the wagons.

"There will be plenty to go around when we get them Indians out of there. Some places ain't safe now, but we'll handle that," he said in a reassuring manner.

"I believe you will," she said with a smile.

"I'm gonna get me a piece of that free land, too," the sergeant said.

"Tell me about it." She loved hearing about his plans. She had never talked to a man so much in her life. And she couldn't imagine talking that long with any other man, but she tried not to think about that. The Oleson brothers might not like all the time they spent together.

"You know," he told her one evening as he walked her back to her coach as the sun was setting, "I've never been able to talk to any other woman like I can talk with you."

She laughed. "You are so tall and handsome that women must flutter around you and want to talk with you all the time."

He laughed at that. "No, but I sure am glad that you don't mind sitting and talking with me most evenings."

"I enjoy it." She smiled up at him. "And I feel much safer with you around."

Pausing their walk, he turned to her and took her hand and held it between his. "Katrin, I gotta tell you that I don't want to think about you coming all the way out here to marry someone else. I just found you. I don't want to have to give you away when we get to where we're going and you find the brothers you're promised to."

"What are you saying?" she asked softly.

"You're the woman I want to be my wife, not someone else's."

"Oh, Tavis. Do you really mean that?"

"Yes, and in six months when I can leave the Army, I'm going to homestead and prove up so we will own our own land. I'll build a house to keep us all nice and warm, and we'll farm the land. I grew up on a farm in Scotland and I'm not afraid of hard work."

"I don't know what to say. I want so much to be a part of your family picture, Tavis, but…"

"Then, will you marry me, Katrin?" he blurted out, not letting her finish. "Tell me you will, lass."

"Oh, Tavis, I want to. But how can I? I'm promised to one of the Oleson brothers."

The smile disappeared from his face. "I know, but now that I know you want to marry me, we just have to figure out a way so you can."

She threw her arms around his neck and kissed him on the cheek. He hugged her and then kissed her on the lips. He'd never kissed her before, and she liked the way it made her feel warm all over.

"We'll find a way. I know we will," Tavis promised.

She wanted to believe that they would.

* * * *

When the rain started again during the night, the soldiers who had been sleeping outside got cold and wet quickly. They grabbed the blankets they had been lying on and moved to get into the shelter of a wagon or coach. The overloading was not much of a problem, because the lightning and thunder made it impossible for anyone to sleep. It rained hard enough to put out some of the campfires that had been lit the night before to illuminate the campsite. The cook did his best to keep the cooking fire going, but it sputtered and smoked and went out just as if he had thrown a pail of water directly on it.

With Alice and Rose's husbands crowded into Anna's coach, the women all gave up trying to sleep. Though the boys wouldn't admit it, the others could see the lightning frightened them. Anna and Katrin moved to give Eric room to sit between them. Jethro had a candle in the pack he wore at his waist. He lit it and the boys felt better.

"See there? The light outside ain't so bright with a light inside, too," Jethro told the boys.

The children leaned against the adults and were soon asleep again despite the noise of the storm. Jethro blew out the candle to save it and the coach was lit only by the raging storm.

Anna took hold of Elsie's hand. It felt cold. "With as hard as the rain is coming down, it can't last too long," Anna said in a low voice so she wouldn't wake the boys. But for all she knew, a storm could last for days out there. Letters from the Oleson brothers had said that the snowstorms in the winter lasted for days, but they hadn't mentioned rainstorms.

"I'll be all right," Elsie said softly with an attempt at a smile.

"I bet we'll all wish we could sleep later in the morning," Alice said, leaning her head on her husband's shoulder.

"If we get a chance to sleep at all," he replied. "The lieutenant will want to move on as soon as it's light."

The rain turned to a quieter but steady downpour after about an hour. By then their exhaustion had caught up with them, and most of the inhabitants of the coach were asleep where they sat. Anna helped Elsie lean down with her head on Anna's lap and her feet up on the strap seat in the middle of the coach. Feeling that her hands were still like ice, Anna took her own coat off and opened it to spread over the older woman.

"Bless you, my dear," Elsie murmured. "God bless you."

As the light of day woke the pioneers, they exited the coach to find a soaking wet campsite.

"Elsie's still asleep," Anna, the last to leave the coach, whispered as she climbed down to the wet grass. "I moved your bag over to support her head when I got up."

"Good. We can leave her to sleep as long as she can before the coach is ready to move out," Katrin said. "We'll bring her something to eat while we're moving."

The others agreed and moved away to conduct their morning ablutions. Their breakfast was damp cold biscuits and a piece of bacon for each of them left from the day before. The cook had managed to get a small fire going with wood he had under cover on his wagon and that allowed him to have pots of hot coffee ready. Welcomed by all the travelers, a steaming cup of the brew went a long way to warming them up.

The blankets the men had slept on under the wagons were soaked from the rain. Wherever they could, they tied them on the sides of the wagons so they could dry as they rode. The saddle blankets had to go back on the horses wet, however. The saddles were wet, too, and squeaked more than usual when the men mounted.

When the coaches and wagons began to move out, the lieutenant rode to the coach where Eric and the women stood outside. "Aren't you all ready to go?" he asked.

"We're giving Elsie a few minutes longer to sleep. I don't think she slept at all last night," Anna explained.

The lieutenant nodded. "Thank you, but we must move out." He dismounted and opened the door of the coach. "Elsie," he called with a gentle voice. "It's time for us to get moving. Can we help you out to…"

He stopped talking and stepped up into the coach. He lifted Elsie's hand and felt her wrist before he laid his hand over her cheek. Kneeling next to her, he put his ear right over her mouth and then listened to her chest. Straightening and slowly shaking his head, he backed out of the coach.

Anna had been at the door watching. "Is she…"

The lieutenant nodded. "I was hoping she'd make it to the fort, but everything was too much for her."

"What's wrong, Pa?" Eric asked, moving past Anna to see what was happening. "Is Grandmother sick?"

The lieutenant closed the coach door. He picked up Eric and held him. "No, son. I'm sorry, but this trip was just too much for her. She passed some time during the night."

"No, Pa, she couldn't die. She said she wanted to go all the way to Dakota Territory with me. We have plans. We have things we're going to do when we get there."

"I'm sorry, son," the lieutenant said.

Eric put his arms around his father's neck and hugged him hard and cried.

"I have to find my sergeant. We'll have to bury her here."

"I see where the sergeant is," Katrin put in. "I can run get him and tell him what happened. You stay with Eric."

"Yes, Lieutenant, why don't you take Eric for a little walk? He needs you to be with him now," Anna added.

Adam nodded and turned away, hugging Eric to his chest.

Katrin ran to the sergeant who stopped the wagon train when he heard the news. She came back riding behind him on his horse, her arms wrapped tightly around his waist. He lifted a leg over the horse's neck and jumped to the ground before lifting her down, too. Katrin had already explained to him what happened. He tied his horse to a ring mounted on the rear of the coach and walked to where the lieutenant was standing talking to Eric.

"Where, sir?" he asked.

"We think the rise there by the tall pines would be nice, right, Eric?" the lieutenant said.

"Yes," the boy said barely above a whisper.

The sergeant saluted and returned to assign three men to digging the grave. Word passed through the wagon train quickly. Several women came to offer their help. They moved Elsie onto a stretcher made by wrapping an Army blanket around two poles. The women straightened her hair and buttoned her coat.

"Do you know," one asked hesitantly," if she has anything with her that she would want to keep for Eric?"

Anna shook her head. “I never saw her wear jewelry except her wedding ring. Let me go ask the lieutenant.”

She met him returning with Eric. The boy had stopped crying and was acting as bravely as a five year old could.

“I’m sorry, but her wedding ring? Do you want that for Eric to have?”

The lieutenant set Eric on the ground and ran his hand through his hair before replacing his hat. “Thank you. That’s a good idea.”

“Is there anything else she might have on her?”

Adam shook his head. “I don’t know, but I don’t think so. All her things are in a trunk in one of the wagons up front. She just had her coat and hat and a blanket.”

“Then we’re ready,” Anna told him.

“Ah, the coat,” Adam said before he moved toward the grave. “Some of the wives are from the south, and they don’t have a good coat of wool like hers. I think she would want one of them to have it.”

With no time to plan a service, it was completely spontaneous. Adam and Eric stood beside the stretcher, which lay beside the grave. Eric looked behind him to find Anna and reached to hold her hand, too. When he tugged on her hand, she moved forward and stood beside them like one of the family.

Other passengers from the stopped wagon train had heard the news and come back to the grave. A few women said how much they admired Elsie for taking on the journey at her age. They concluded that she had done it because she loved Eric so much.

“I loved her, too,” he said in response.

When the soldiers lowered Elsie’s blanket-wrapped body into the grave, Eric began to whimper again. Adam picked him up and walked back toward the circle of wagons with an order to the sergeant to carry on.

When the burial was over and a protective pile of large rocks had been put over the grave, the families went back to their wagons and the soldiers to their horses. More than half the morning was gone. The lieutenant gave the order to move out as soon as everyone was ready. Everyone was soon back in his or her wagon and moving west.

Anna saw Eric's head bobbing as his lack of sleep caught up with him. "Come over here and put your head on my lap," she suggested. He moved to sit next to her and she laid her hand on his shoulder. In moments he was asleep. It didn't take long for the rest of the passengers to follow suit.

For a while as they slept they all escaped their thoughts of Elsie's passing. When they woke, there would be plenty of time to remember and to mourn.

The toll of a death of a family member on the journey was a greater cost than anyone had expected. It was greater than anyone had wanted to pay.

* * * *

The rain gave them only a day to dry out, but when it came back with a vengeance the next night, it didn't give up so easily. The winds rose before the rain and rocked the wagons. Soldiers ran to add more tie-downs to the canvas tops on the covered wagons. The cook welcomed their help in tying down the oiled cloth spread over his food store and over the dry wood he and his assistant had collected the day before. He couldn't cook without a fire and needed to keep the wood dry enough to burn.

By the light of day the next morning it was still raining and puddles of water filled every depression. The ground was too wet to absorb any more water.

When the drivers tried to pull the wagons out of the circle and back onto the road, the wheels sank into the saturated earth. Moving a heavy baggage wagon and the freight wagon loaded with food and goods for the fort was impossible at first. The feat was accomplished only after hitching a second team to the first. Once the wagons were on the road, they unhitched the extra team and led them back to their own wagon.

To make the remaining wagons as light as possible while they moved them back to the packed road, the passengers had to get out and walk despite the rain. By late morning, when all the wagons were finally lined up on the road, every passenger, driver, and soldier was soaked to the skin and mud spattered. The women's skirts weighed many times more than what they had before with the rain and mud-caked hems. When trying to walk, they sometimes slipped in the mud and fell. Once back on their feet, they had only to hold out their muddy hands and skirts to let the heavy rain wash at least some of the mud off.

Afraid of the storm and challenged beyond their strength by the tough walking, the children cried and waited to be picked up. Carrying a child made the walking too hard for some mothers. Seeing a woman who had slipped and fallen, kneeling in the mud with a child in their arms, the sergeant's assistant dismounted and lifted them onto his saddle. He took the reins and led the horse to the road. In a few minutes the woman's husband rode up.

"I can take them now, but thanks," he shouted over the noise of the storm.

The private pointed ahead at another woman finding walking nearly impossible. "I got them. You go get those."

The soldier looked at his wife who sat on the horse sideways with their bent knee over the pommel. Their daughter, with her face buried inside her mother's coat, sat on her mother's lap. Her mother's drooping hat gave her some measure of more protection from the driving rain.

"Go ahead," she shouted. "We're fine here." Her husband rode on to rescue the other woman.

Lightning lit the sky and thunder boomed just a few seconds later. Higher on the hill they were approaching, a tree was hit by the strike and came crashing to the ground. Sparks and flames flew out, but the rain quickly doused them.

The sergeant came to rescue Katrin as she had hoped. Beyond embarrassment, she threw her leg over the saddle after he lifted her up and rode astride with her skirts reaching only barely past her knees. He called an order to a private who stopped and picked up Anna and Eric. Also riding astride, she wrapped her arms around Eric who sat in front of her while they both hung onto the pommel. The private swung up and rode sitting on his bedroll behind the saddle.

Checking on the whole wagon train, the lieutenant rode by. He saw Anna holding Eric firmly and mouthed the words, "Thank you." Anna smiled her response.

"See, Father? I'm riding a horse," Eric announced proudly, blinking the rain out of his eyes as he looked up at his father with a broad grin.

"You're doing just fine, son," his father told him.

Anna smiled as Adam's gaze flitted over her from head to toe, and then rose to meet hers. She was aware that he noticed her bared calf beyond the edge of her stretched skirt. Her skirt wasn't full enough to pull down, so she could do nothing but keep her hold on Eric.

"You can get back in the coach as soon as it gets back onto the road," he said with a smile. His hat brim keeping the rain from his eyes, he rode on.

Once the wagons and coaches all reached the packed road, the passengers rescued on horseback were returned to their respective places inside them. Without exception everyone was cold and wet and muddy again. Shivering, Anna and the others huddled together in their coach.

"I'm cold," Eric admitted.

Seeing that he was shivering and worried he might get sick, she lifted him onto her lap and removed his thoroughly wet coat. Then she unbuttoned her coat so she could hold Eric against her for warmth. He slid his arms around her and leaned against her. Using his blanket, she wrapped it around them like a cocoon.

"I wish I had the mittens that Grandma knitted for me, but they are in her trunk. She said I wouldn't need them in the summer."

"It's good that you will have them when the snow falls."

"She's got all my clothes and other things like books and even dishes and cups and some pots for cooking in her trunk. It takes two men to lift it," he said with a laugh.

"She took good care of you and wanted you to have everything you would need in your new home."

He nodded and tried to stifle a yawn. "I miss her."

"We all do."

He didn't move from the warmth she provided and settled his head between her breasts and soon fell asleep. She looked down at his sweet face and knew that she would miss him terribly when they got to Dakota Territory, and she left the fort with her husband-to-be. She could only hope that they would live near the fort so she could visit Eric. But most likely then she would see his father, too. Seeing him again after marrying another man would not be a good idea.

She leaned her head back and closed her eyes, trying to think of something else.

Chapter 8

The rain lasted two more days. Anna and Katrin thought the farmers in Norway would be happy with the soaking rain at the end of May. The passengers on the wagon train did not welcome it at all. They were fortunate that the nights weren't too cold, because no one managed to dry off for any length of time before they had to get out of the wagons again.

At the noon mealtime when they stopped, the lieutenant had ordered all the drivers to keep their wagons on the road. He wasn't going to spend so much time getting them lined up on the road again. It meant the passengers had to walk a long way from the wagons farthest from the cook's, but they were all wet already.

Alice volunteered to go to the cook wagon to get the food for everyone in her coach. Bringing back what she could carry in a deep pocket formed by folding up the apron she wore, she passed out soggy biscuits and limp bacon to the others. She didn't bother with the tin plates that the cook had for everyone to use. With fewer to wash, he could leave sooner and the wagon train could get on its way again. They all hoped they would ride out of the rain very soon.

"I'm getting tired of eating soggy biscuits. My grandmother used to make them better than this," Eric remarked.

"I think we should be happy we have anything to eat," Alice told him. "Maybe the rain will stop tonight, and the cooks can make a fire tomorrow."

"I hope so," Eric replied. He looked up at Anna, who was sitting beside him because he had taken the seat that Elsie had used. "Don't you?"

"Yes, I think we all do."

After a dull day confined to the coach, except when absolutely necessary, they curled up for the night shortly after supper, and the light of the sun rising woke them in the early morning. Eric rose onto his hands and knees on the bench where he had slept and looked out the window. "It's not raining," he said brightly. "But look, the grass is all on fire."

"What?" the women cried in unison as they moved to pull back the fabric coverings over the windows and look out themselves. They laughed when they saw what he was referring to.

"It's not smoke, Eric," Anna told him. "It's moisture from the rain rising from the wet ground. Look at the lake over there. See it rising like steam from a kettle over the water, too?"

"I never saw anything like that before," he said.

They all climbed out of the wagon and went about their morning routines, happy to only get their feet and the hems of their skirts wet.

"I wish we could wash these muddy clothes before moving on," Anna said, looking down at her spattered and stained skirt.

"Exactly what I thought," a deep voice said behind her.

Knowing it was Adam, she smiled and turned to him.

"Father, did you see the grass this morning? I thought it was on fire and smoking, but Miss Anna said it wasn't," Eric said.

The lieutenant met Anna's gaze. "Miss Anna is a good teacher. You would do well to listen to her."

"She tells good stories, too. I was a little scared of the lightning, and she told me stories so I wouldn't think about it."

"Thank you, Miss Anna," Adam said with a warm smile.

"When are we going to start out, Father?"

"As soon as everyone is ready. We all need some time to wash the mud from the clothes we've been wearing during the storm."

"But we don't have a line to hang them on like Grandma had at home," Eric pointed out. "How will they dry?"

The lieutenant looked at the coach. I guess you'll have to hang them from the coach. We tried it with the soldiers' blankets and it worked. They dry as we go. I don't think we'll get more rain today."

Eric laughed. "Our coach will have flowered flags with the women's dresses hanging on it. That'll look funny."

"I think so too, Eric," Anna told him. "But the thought of getting this dress clean of all the mud makes me want to do it."

She and the others took turns changing their clothes in the coach and then waited for their turn to use the washtubs that some had brought with them. A lake always seemed to be close by as they traveled, and the soldiers carried pails full of water as it was needed. With no dry wood to burn, they didn't take the time to heat it, but even washing them in cold water was better than not washing them at all. And they did have the soap from Tavis, so the sisters weren't afraid to use the bar they brought with them even though it was getting thin.

"I'm thankful some folks had tin wash tubs tied on their wagons," Alice said as she wrung out her dress. "The one I had back home in the mountains was made of wood. It leaked at first, but when I filled it, the water would swell the wood and then it would stay in it." She shook out her dress. "There. I'm done, so it's your turn and thanks for letting me use the soap," she added to Katrin.

Alice went to hang up her dress to dry. Katrin washed hers and handed the bar of soap to Anna. Katrin rinsed her hands and hung up her dress to dry.

"I like having the soap, but we never should have accepted the gift of soap," Anna put in.

"I think it was sweet of him to help us by giving it to us," Katrin countered.

"I can guess who gave it to you," Alice said with a laugh as she finished tying her dress on the door.

Katrin felt the heat creep up into her cheeks. "I…I…"

"You've got a good man there," Alice concluded. "And he's a smart one. He knows a woman could never say no to a bar of soap." She laughed. "Come on, Jimmy. Let's go find your father and see what he wants washed. He's only got the one uniform, but he might want his socks scrubbed."

"I'm going to wash all my stockings, too," Katrin said as Anna finished washing her dress a few minutes later. "I've been wearing two pairs each day and they all need a good scrubbing since we've been walking ankle deep in mud."

"Good idea. I'll go get mine," Anna said as she draped her dress over the bar that kept the luggage in place on top of the coach. She brought the sleeves down and tied them over the front of the dress to keep it from falling off. "A few months ago I would have been very embarrassed by drying my dress on a coach where everyone could see it. Today I'm too happy to have clean clothes to even worry about."

"That reason, and because every other wagon and coach is decorated the same way," Katrin added. The sisters both laughed and went on scrubbing their stockings. They still had Eric's trousers and socks to wash, too.

A soldier came over to see if they were done with the tub. "I thought the lieutenant might let us stay here a day to do the wash and to let it dry out," Katrin said as they finished their wash.

The soldier dumped the muddy water. "Really not my place to say, Ma'am, but I don't think he wants to spend any more time on the road than necessary with them Indian bands out there up to no good."

"I think you're right," Anna told him.

"Thanks for your help with the tub," Katrin added before he returned the washtub to the owner and helped him lash it on the side of the covered wagon.

Some of the soldiers had no clothes to change into from their muddy ones. They solved the dilemma by walking into the nearby lake. Swimming or just splashing around resulted in cleaner clothes and a cooler soldier in the humid early summer heat.

And much to everyone's amazement, Enid and Alfred, who had done so well with their hunting skills, showed the families they knew how to fish, too. Moving away from the noisy bathers who had muddied the water, they unwound fishing lines with hooks that they wore around the brim of their hats. It didn't take long before they plucked out enough large pike that the cook fried up nicely for dinner with the flapjacks. There was some venison left, too, and the cook crushed wild berries picked from patches beside their route with honey for a delicious topping for the feast.

The party atmosphere of such a delicious and different dinner continued when the scouts that the lieutenant had sent on ahead reported back.

"We're only a week away from the fort," they said.

Everyone cheered. They were almost home.

"Being that close does not mean we can let our guard down," the lieutenant reminded them. "Keep your eyes open, your rifles loaded, and be prepared for anything. We have to remain on guard, because we don't know what's out there."

Knowing they were close made the traveling seem easier. The biscuits and slices of venison fried in bacon fat for breakfast the next day seemed tasty and special, because the biscuits weren't soggy. The pot of beans that accompanied almost every meal was hot and much more inviting that it had been during the storms when the cook could not get a big fire going.

As the day progressed, walking beside the wagons no longer seemed like such a tiring way to travel. Drinks of water from the barrels that the soldiers filled when they could from lakes they passed didn't taste as muddy. The sun shone and not a rain cloud marred the blue sky.

Everyone was still in such a happy mood that next evening—everyone except Anna, Katrin, and even Eric. The closer the sisters got to their destination the more they regretted their promise. They ate their dinner with Eric, Adam and Tavis as they did most nights. The men had left to check on the horses and assign the guards who would take turns during the night.

"Did you notice anything strange about Eric today?" Anna asked her sister softly so Eric could not hear her. Katrin shook her head. "He's been so quiet all day and I don't know why."

"You're right, and look at him now. He's just throwing broken pieces of that twig he's breaking up onto the fire. He hasn't been interested in any of the games or activities that Jimmy suggested before we ate."

"I hope he's not getting sick."

"Eric, there's a little time before we go back to the coach for the night," Anna called. "Don't you feel like playing your stick game with Jimmy?"

He shook his head.

She walked over to him and felt his forehead, but couldn't detect how much heat was his and how much was caused by sitting close to the fire. "Do you feel well?"

"I suppose."

"You seem sad. What are you sad about?"

He looked up at Anna, then to Katrin and back again. "I was just thinking. We're getting close to the fort."

She nodded.

"What are you going to do when you get to the fort?" he asked.

"Take a bath," the sisters said without hesitation. They laughed, but Eric did not.

"No, I mean…well, Father said you came here to marry two men from Norway who are already there."

"Yes, Eric," Anna said. "We promised their uncle to come here to marry the Oleson brothers. We told you how they came here before we did. They've already settled in Dakota Territory and built homes somewhere that we will live in."

"No, I don't want you to. If you do, I may never see you again," he blurted out, throwing the rest of the branch in the fire.

"Oh, I would hate for that to happen, too, and I don't think it will," Anna said. "You'll be living at the fort with your father, and I'll see you every time I go there."

He jumped to his feet and faced her with his hands on his hips. "But I want you to marry my father. Then you could always be with us." He lowered his head and his lower lip jutted out in a pout.

Anna knelt and put her arms around the boy and hugged him. She pressed her lips together to keep from saying that she wanted that, too. "I'm sorry, Eric," she did say. "But I can promise that I will always be your friend." She glanced up to see Katrin with tears glistening in her eyes.

"I would like to have you for my friend," Eric said, looking like he felt better about the situation.

"And I would like very much to have you for my friend." Anna rose and brushed imagined grass from her skirt as she worked at getting a smile on her face. "Now, why don't you go play with Jimmy? It's almost time to bed down, but I'll call you."

Eric nodded and walked toward one of the other campfires where his friend Jimmy sat with his parents.

Katrin rose from the log they had been sitting on and stepped close beside her. "Anna, I'm going to marry Tavis," she said before Anna had a chance to speak. "I love him, and I can't marry one of the Oleson brothers. I just can't."

"You can't or won't? What about your promise?" Anna asked.

Tears overflowed and rolled down Katrin's cheeks. "I don't know. They may hate me, but I just can't. I won't." She turned and walked toward the sergeant who Anna saw walking toward them from the corral.

Anna didn't want to watch them. They talked each night and seemed so happy together. She didn't want to see the smiles on their faces as Katrin put her hands into his that he held out to her. She didn't want to see them leave for their evening walk. She turned her back and stepped beyond the circle of wagons a few steps to be out of sight of the rest. Feeling very alone and lonely, she tipped her head up and looked at the stars shining so brightly. They blurred into a sparkling cover high above her when tears filled her own eyes. Heaven help her, she didn't want to marry one of the Oleson brothers either. What were she and Katrin going to do? She couldn't see that they had much choice—not if they were to keep their promises.

"Star gazing?" Adam asked as he stepped up close behind her and laid his hands on each side of her waist.

She whirled around and wrapped her arms around his neck. "Oh, Adam, I can't bear the thought of losing you," she told him. "I know I shouldn't be so bold as to say so, but I can't help myself."

"Anna, I'm glad to hear you say it, because I want you in my life permanently. But we have no choice. You made a promise." His warm hands stroked up and down her back, but she wasn't comforted.

"Yes, but when I made it, I didn't know I would meet you." She straightened so her gaze could meet his. "I've come to care a great deal for you and for your son."

"And you know we care for you, but your promise was a promise—a matter of honor."

"I know," she said, choking back a sob as he pulled her back in his arms. They clung to each other, knowing it was too near to being the last time they could be alone together like this. The kisses they shared moments later were bittersweet. They were goodbye kisses.

A matter of honor was keeping them apart.

But his deep sense of honor was one of the attributes that made Anna love him.

* * * *

The sun shone brightly as they neared the end of one of the last days in their trek across Minnesota. The cook had served a hot meal of fried ham and flapjacks with berries. The soldiers didn't allow folks to go too far from the wagon train, but they found enough berries close by the road to give them all a taste. When the bell rang announcing that supper was ready, the soldiers ate with their families, almost forgetting that they should be on the lookout for Indians.

After breaking their fast at first light, the soldiers got ready and saddled their horses as their families got settled in their wagons. Chores were quickly done, because they all knew they didn't have to ride in the bumpy wagons for much longer.

The lieutenant gave the signal to begin. Other soldiers passed it down the row as they had done for the whole journey. Many of the men waved to their wives and children before taking their position along side the wagon train as it pulled out onto the road.

They hadn't been on the road for long when a gunshot was heard from near the front of the wagon train followed by a woman's scream and children's cries. One of the covered wagons stopped suddenly. The drivers behind them managed to also stop quickly only by turning the horses to the side of the road and pulling hard on the reins while they shouted at them to whoa. The continued screams of the woman were heard over the drivers' shouts at the horses and the soldier's shouts to be on the lookout for whoever had just shot at the wagon train.

When the sisters' coach was stopped and the brake set, Jake jumped down from the coach and talked to the horses to calm them.

"Why are we stopped?" Eric asked.

"I don't know, but they'll tell us soon enough," Anna said with a smile so he wouldn't worry.

"All the soldiers are riding up there. I can go with them find out," he volunteered eagerly.

"I think you'd better stay with us." Anna looked at Rose who had opened the door to stand on the step for a better viewpoint. "Can you see anything?"

"Folks are gathering near a covered wagon up front, but I can't see well with the wagons turned all over the roadway." She jumped down to the ground. "I'll go see what it is."

"I'll go with you," Katrin offered. She jumped down, too, and the two women headed forward past the stopped wagons along with several others.

The lieutenant rode up from the rear and shouted to the men to return to their guard posts beside the wagons. Several pulled their reins to the side and rode back along the wagons.

"Don't leave your posts!" he added. He reined his horse between two askew wagons and rode back the other side to get the men back into position there. Once they were in place, he headed forward to see what the gunshot was about.

Katrin and Rose joined the circle of onlookers ahead of him and gasped at what they saw.

A little boy, not any bigger than Eric, lay on the road. A stain of blood was growing on his trouser leg and spreading in a circle on the packed earth beneath him. Feeling helpless, they watched as the boy's mother cradled his head in her lap and cried. "No, Tommy, oh God, no." Her tears fell to the boy's face, but he didn't react. "Help him! Somebody help him," she cried.

"Ma, we want to get down. What's wrong with Tommy?" two older girls called from the covered wagon that had stopped several yards down the road. A soldier dismounted and helped the girls to the ground and they ran to their mother's side.

"Mommy, mommy," they cried. "Why is Tommy bleeding?"

"Oh no, it's Tommy," Rose whispered. "He's played with Jimmy and Eric some, but look at him. He's covered with blood."

"What happened?" Katrin asked a woman near them.

She shook her head. "I don't know, but here comes his father."

A soldier rode to the scene from the front of the wagon train and leapt from his horse. "Tommy! What is it? How'd he get hurt?" Tommy's father asked as he knelt by his son. He touched the blood spreading on the boy's pant leg and looked at his fingers as if he didn't believe they were red. "Where's all this blood from?"

"Mommy, I'm cold," the boy said weakly.

"Tommy, what happened?" his father cried, but the boy didn't answer.

One of the soldiers who had just arrived on the scene knelt opposite Tommy's father. "Help me get the boy's trousers off. We gotta find out what happened and stop the bleeding."

They did that and saw a gaping wound on the inside of his thigh. Blood poured from the wound in rhythmic pulses and dripped onto the earth beneath him. The soldier pulled off his neck scarf, crumpled it into a ball, and pressed it on the wound.

"No, stop." Tommy moaned. "Mama, it hurts." His head tossed from one side to the other.

"Gimme yours to hold this in place," he said to the boy's father. "We gotta stop the bleeding."

The father took his kerchief from around his neck and tied it around Tommy's leg to hold the other one in place. The other soldier kept pressure on the wound by pressing on it.

"What happened?" the lieutenant, who rode up and jumped from his horse, asked. He handed the reins to another soldier and walked to Tommy's father's side. "Did anyone see what happened?"

"The boy took a bullet in the leg. It cut the artery I'm afraid," the soldier trying to stem the bleeding said. "When that happens, I seen enough like that to know there's no stopping 'em."

All color left the boy's face and his head slumped to the side. His eyes stared, seeing nothing.

"I'm sorry, but there was nothing more anyone could do."

"Tommy," his father shouted. "Tommy!"

"No," his mother wailed and several women standing by openly wept.

"How did he get shot?" the lieutenant asked. "Where'd the bullet come from?" He looked at a few soldiers who had gathered with the families instead of staying on guard duty.

"We saw no one, sir," the soldiers agreed, shaking their heads.

Everyone looked to the mother for answers. Still crying and holding her dead son, the boy's mother managed, "I don't know how it happened. They were playing in the wagon when he got up and went toward the back. That's where the pot is for the kids to use so we don't have to stop so often. I thought he was going there."

The lieutenant looked at the boy's father.

"I was riding up front. I came after I heard the gun shot like everyone else."

The lieutenant rose and looked at the soldiers still standing there. "Men, keep your eyes open for anyone along the road who could have shot the boy."

The men obeyed his order and climbed into their saddles, but before they could leave, the driver of the next wagon stepped forward.

"Lieutenant, I was driving the team following theirs, and I can tell ya that the lad had one leg over the back and looked like he was going to climb down. Then he lost his hold and fell off the wagon. I was glad there was enough space between my team and him so I could move off the road instead of riding over him. He would have been trampled under my horse's hooves."

"But he's been shot. How did he get shot?" the lieutenant asked the driver, exasperation evident in his voice.

"It all seemed to happen at once. He leaned over to get a grip with his hands to climb down, and then I heard the shot and he fell. But I didn't know he was shot until I stopped my wagon and got over here."

"We told him never to climb off a moving wagon," the boy's father insisted. "He was to wait until it stopped." He turned to his wife. "Did you know he was getting down?"

She shook her head. "No, no. We were all in the wagon and then he was gone."

"But the shot? How did he get shot?" the lieutenant asked, getting more impatient that the questions about what had happened were taking so long and getting so few answers at such a time.

"This might be the reason," the soldier who had tried to stop the bleeding said. He had walked over toward the covered wagon to get a scoop of water from the barrel to wash his hands. He picked up a revolver from the high grass between the worn wheel paths in the road. He handed it to the Lieutenant who examined it. The gun was loaded and one bullet had been fired.

"Let me see that," the father said, taking it from him. "That's mine. I made these carvings on the handle." He reached for his wife's upper arm, grasped it hard, and shook her. "What was he doing with my revolver? How did he get it?" His wife, bent over her dead son, burst into tears again and couldn't speak.

"Easy, soldier," the lieutenant said firmly as he leaned down and took the revolver from his hand before it went off again.

Tommy's mother raised her head. "He sees you putting it away after you clean it. He knew where it was," she managed to tell her husband.

"I had to put it where I could reach it from horseback if there was trouble," he insisted.

"Looks like he took it and maybe tucked it in his belt," the other soldier offered. "I've seen revolvers go off in a belt when a man just bent down. If the boy was climbing down the gun could have hit the side or caught in his belt and gone off."

The lieutenant handed the gun to the soldier who had found it. "See that he puts this away when he can." He turned to the others who had gathered and asked the women to help prepare the boy for burial. "And assign two or three men to dig a grave," he told the sergeant who was standing by as usual.

Death wasn't a stranger to any of the soldier's families. While several of the families, as well as Katrin and Rose, returned to their wagons, a few of the women who knew the family better than the others stayed. They helped Tommy's mother to stand and get into her wagon with her daughters. There they helped her wash and change her skirt that was stained with blood. The girls cried and sat close, not understanding all that was happening.

Outside the wagon, the boy's father carried him to a grassy area beyond the wagons. A soldier friend of his brought two pails of water and two other women quietly worked together to bathe the boy. They dressed him in clean clothes that his father had brought to them from the wagon. As the mother, the boy's sisters, and his father stood by, two soldiers lifted him and wrapped him in the blanket that he had slept under each night of their journey.

The lieutenant walked over when a soldier told him that they were ready. "Is the spot on that rise overlooking the lake all right?" the lieutenant asked Tommy's father.

"It don't matter. My boy is gone. Don't matter where you put him."

The lieutenant gave the soldiers who had gotten the shovels a signal to carry on. "Seems he must have wanted to help guard his mother and his sisters. Don't you think he was climbing out to keep watch and help the soldiers?"

Tommy's father looked at him a moment and then away. "I don't know, but that makes sense. He didn't like being stuck inside with his sisters, but I told him a hundred times not to touch the revolver."

"Finding a different place to keep it safe…"

"I know. I put it in my saddlebag. It's handy there for me, but I thought that keeping it in the wagon would give my wife some protection if she needed it. That and this rifle is all we got."

"We're almost to the fort." The lieutenant looked at the rise to the south of the road ahead. "And Tommy can keep watch from on the hill."

"Yes, sir. I guess he could. He'd like that."

The lieutenant nodded and went to tell the sergeant to inform everyone that the service would begin as soon as the grave was dug.

The families, drivers, and soldiers all gathered for the short service as they had for Elsie's. Anger was still evident in the manner the boy's father treated his wife. They had lost so much in the war and now they had lost their only son. He ignored his two older daughters who clung to their mother as he walked straight to his horse after the grave was covered. His family climbed into their covered wagon with others to assist them. Unable to do more, the rest of the mourners went back to their respective wagons and coaches.

"Move out as you are ready," the lieutenant shouted to the drivers as he rode down the line. When he got to Eric's coach he stopped and dismounted. Eric was standing beside the coach with Jimmy and the women.

"How come Tommy died, Father? He wasn't old like Grandmother."

Adam squatted down beside his son. "No, he wasn't and he shouldn't have died. He did something very foolish. He took his father's gun when he'd been told never to touch it."

"Is that why you told me never to touch yours? So I wouldn't die?"

"That's exactly why. I lost your mother. My heart would break if I ever lost you." He hugged Eric and then rose. Keeping his hand on the boy's shoulder, he looked at Anna.

Anna returned his gaze and knew that they were thinking that their hearts would break when they had to part after finding the Oleson brothers.

Adam helped Anna into the coach and lifted Eric up to the step, too, before mounting his horse and checking on the rest of the wagon train.

"Get on in, Jimmy," Rose said, but she didn't make any move to get in after him. She lifted the corner of the apron that she wore to keep her skirt clean and wiped her forehead.

Katrin, waiting her turn to climb in, asked, "Are you all right, Rose? You look a little pale."

"Being in the fresh air is better than that stuffy coach. My stomach is just churning a bit this morning, but I'm much better now." She smiled and climbed in.

Jake looked down from his perch and asked if they were all ready.

"Soon as I get in," Katrin told him.

He nodded and took up the reins. One by one the wagons and coaches pulled back into an orderly line with a safe amount of space between them. They moved west on their journey that had exacted the price of yet another life.

Chapter 9

The next several mornings Katrin couldn't help but notice that Rose didn't look well. She often stayed in the wagon to lie down while the others went to break their fast. They would bring her what they could for her to eat, but she never touched it until it was time to stop at noon or even later.

"Do you think we should tell Jethro?" Katrin asked Anna. "She's not eating and she's napping all the time. She's acting like Elsie did before she died."

"I checked, and she doesn't have a fever. She told me not to worry," Anna replied.

"Jethro never sees her except late afternoon and the overnights when they could sleep outside together before we were told to stay in the coach. I've never heard him say anything appeared to be wrong."

"I don't know what to do, but I think that if she is ill for one more day, we should say something to her about telling Jethro," Katrin said. "He could at least comfort her."

"Good," Anna agreed.

The next morning, Rose was ill enough to eject the contents of her stomach. Backing away from there, she knelt in the grass for a few minutes.

Katrin walked to her side. "Rose, tell me what we can do for you. You're getting sicker as the days pass."

Rose surprised her by looking up and smiling. "That is so sweet of you, but believe me there is nothing you can do for me."

"Should I get Jethro? If you're too weak to walk, he could carry you to the coach."

Rose laughed lightly and stood up. "Honey, he already done enough."

Katrin frowned. Seeing her frown, Rose laughed.

"I have never seen anyone so ill who thinks it is so funny."

"No, it's not funny. It's wonderful!" Rose said. "We couldn't be happier."

Katrin stopped and reached for Rose's arm to stop her. Anna was only a few feet from them at the side of the coach and stepped closer.

"All right, Rose. What is going on? Just why are you so happy at being so sick?"

Rose shook her head, a big grin still on her face. "I'm not sick. I am with child."

Katrin's mouth dropped open and Anna smiled.

"But you've been so sick to your stomach," Katrin put in.

"It's like that for some women, but it will pass in another week or two."

"We didn't know," Katrin said.

"I didn't know either, that I was going to have a baby, I mean, until Jethro told me that my breasts…well, he said they were getting bigger. That's when I figured it out. I figured I had missed my monthlies just because of the stress of this traveling."

"Oh, dear. There's a lot we have to learn," Anna added, her cheeks burning at the mention of her swelling breasts and missed monthlies. Neither were things she considered topics of conversation.

"Oh, dear, I can see from the look on your faces that I've shocked you. Sorry, but we're going to be living in the middle of nowhere and I think all women should know what is going on. You have any questions just ask." She laughed suddenly. "My mama didn't feel that way. She didn't want me to know anything about anything before I was married. She said my husband would teach me all I had to know."

Katrin looked at Anna with a wry smile. "That's what our mother told us before we left Norway."

Rose put an arm around each of the sister's waists and steered them toward the coach. "Then I can tell that we will have a lot to talk about. Alice might want to talk with us, too, but we'll have to do it when the boys are not nearby. I'm not ready for Jimmy to learn this when he's so young. He can wait, and then his father can tell him," she said, the grin still on her face.

"Ladies? Ready to leave?" Jake called from his bench seat.

The ladies waved and scrambled up the steps into the coach. As soon as they shut the door, Jake shouted at the horses and got them into motion.

* * * *

The wagon train left the gently rolling hills of the lake-dotted landscape of Minnesota and rode into the flat and wide ancient valley of the Red River. The lieutenant announced at supper that the wagon train would cross the Red River the next day.

"It will be easy to distinguish the Red River from others we have crossed, because the Red flows north. This will be the last big physical challenge the wagon train will face. Our drivers are experienced from bringing supplies to the fort on previous trips. They know the best place to enter the water. I'm letting them lead us to the place on the shore where they wanted to cross."

As they neared the river, the drivers pulled the wagons to a stop in the row and jumped down to walk to the riverbank. The lieutenant and the sergeant joined them.

"It ain't supposed to be this high," one said to the others.

"This is nearly the end of the month of May," another said.

"It's lower than if it was filled with snowmelt earlier in the spring," a third said. "But that's all the good I can say about it."

"The spring flood sure piled debris along the shore," Jake added.

The lieutenant slid from his saddle and watched the fast flow. "Is this where you want to cross?"

One driver took his hat off, pushed his long hair back, and then replaced his hat to hold it in place. "We thought it would be, but there's a lot of deadwood that has to be cleared before we can cross. We can't drive the wagons over all that."

"It looks fast and deep," the lieutenant said. "You're sure it's not too deep?"

"It's more than we expected, but if you can take the women and children across on horseback, then we'll worry about getting the wagons over."

"I'll assign some men to get it done." While the drivers stayed at the riverbank a few minutes longer to agree on how they would cross, the lieutenant and the sergeant passed the word about needing to carry the people across on horseback. The families climbed from the wagons and stood near the bank, waiting their turn.

Several soldiers were soon pulling branches and fallen trees out of the way. A few were so large that they had to lash a rope on them and let the strength of their horses move them out of the way.

When the east bank was clear, the soldiers rode into the river to cross to the other side to complete the job over there. The swift water slapped at the chests of the horses and frightened them. When they weren't allowed to turn around and get out of the water, they lifted both front feet in awkward leaps instead of walking across.

Two soldiers, who had pulled their feet out of the stirrups to keep their boots dry, lost their seat and one ended in the water while another hung on to the pommel and lay on the horse's back, where he was bounced up and down with each leap. Fortunately, the soldier who had fallen into the river surfaced next to another horse. The soldier in the saddle leaned down, grabbed his sleeve, and pulled him to the far shore. The wet soldier's horse had already made it across, but had run far enough that two other soldiers had to ride after him and herd him back to the shore. The soldiers tied all their horses securely to nearby trees so they wouldn't take off while they worked.

When the soldiers had cleaned up the west bank, they stayed there and helped do what they could without crossing back. The women and children were lifted one at a time onto the soldiers' horses for the ride across. The children were excited and most found the trip to be great fun. The women were not so happy about it. They lifted their feet to keep them dry and that threatened the loss of their seat. They clung to the soldier in the saddle in front of them and hoped for the best. They got across without incident. There the sergeant told them to walk toward the road on the rise to the west so they would be out of the way now that the wagons were going to make the crossing. From the shore it was easy to find the well-worn road that trappers had marked decades before, going north to the Winnipeg fur market. Since then, wagons had packed the earth in two parallel lines under their wheels.

"Ingor must have traveled on this road to take his furs to sell them," Anna suggested to Katrin.

"He may not live far from the road then," she replied.

The sisters sat in the grass and waited with the others as the reality sank in of how close they might be from meeting the men they had promised to marry.

The drivers moved the wagons one at a time into the water, going into the flow at a southwesterly direction and stayed at that angle as much as possible until they made it to the west bank. There the slope was not great enough to warrant hitching two teams together to get the wagons up. The single teams worked hard, but even the heaviest wagon made it up. In turn the drivers took their wagons a short distance toward the grassy area beside the road. There they allowed the horses to rest while the remaining wagons forded the river. After crossing, each driver carefully checked the straps and chains on their team of horses to be sure nothing had broken or come loose.

As soon as the cook got his wagon across, he pulled it near where the families were all waiting and began preparing their noon meal. Some of the children had found wild strawberries growing in the grass and more near the trees along the shore. The cook organized them to pick all they could and all the families and drivers enjoyed the tart treat folded in flapjacks.

The cook barely had time to fold up his cabinet in the wagon before the lieutenant ordered the wagon trail to head north. The families watched the landscape as they rode. They were getting close to where they lived, and they were pleasantly surprised by how soon they reached the Wahpeton settlement. Friendly folks, eager to talk to newcomers, came out of their houses and waved as they walked toward the wagon train.

Knowing the families and the soldiers would benefit from talking to residents of the area, the lieutenant rode to the front wagon and ordered the driver's to stop. "Stay in line. We won't stop for long."

One of the women from the settlement came right over to the wagons, "Any of you women school teachers?" she called out as she walked down the line.

The women and children climbed out of the wagons and coaches as soon as they stopped. Their responses were all in the negative because Anna did not answer. However, she had heard the question and wondered if this was a place she could teach if she lived nearby.

Suddenly she gasped and covered her mouth with her fingers.

"What's wrong?" Katrin asked.

"Heavens!" she exclaimed. "One or both of the Oleson brothers might live right here."

"I wish I knew what they look like. I could talk to them and I wouldn't know it."

Anna looked to see that the lieutenant was talking to his men and the drivers who had gathered near the cook's wagon for a cup of cold coffee while they waited. If anyone were going to ask the men and women approaching the wagons about the brothers, it would be her or Katrin.

"I was hoping you have a teacher with you," a woman from the Wahpeton settlement said as she approached the sisters. "My name is Sarah and I've got three kids I'd love to see in school."

Anna introduced her sister and herself to the woman. "I was going to be a teacher if I had stayed in Norway. But I am going to get married here, and my sister, too. So I don't think I will be teaching at all."

"That's too bad, about not teaching here, not about getting married," Sarah said with a laugh. "When's the wedding?"

Anna glanced at Katrin and then looked back at the woman. "We're not sure. We have to find the men we will marry."

The woman laughed again. "That's good news. There's a lot of men around here who will be happy to hear you two are looking for husbands. There aren't many single women here.

"Oh, no," Katrin put in. "We are not looking for husbands like that. We promised to marry the Oleson brothers. I meant we have to find them, because we don't know where they settled out here."

"Have you heard of Ingor and Lars Oleson?" Anna asked.

"Oleson, you say?" She shook her head as she thought about it. "No, can't say as I have." She turned and called to a woman talking to a few other travelers. "Hey, Gertie, have you ever heard of the Oleson brothers? These two," she went on with a sweep of her arm toward Anna and Katrin, "are looking for 'em."

"Isn't one of them the fella who got his cabin burned down a while back? I think his place used to be northwest of the fort. Haven't heard tell of him since then."

"His cabin was burned down? Was he injured?" Anna asked Gertie, anxious to hear her answer.

"Don't know if he was hurt. The cabin burning was all we heard about."

"Oh, dear," Anna said weakly. Her expectations of a completed home ready to move into vanished. What would they do now?

"Well, don't do any good to worry 'bout it until you get all the details. He coulda built another one by now, and it might not even be him at all."

"Of course," Anna said. "That makes me feel a measure better."

"These homes here are not what I expected," Katrin said, looking at the structures in a row several yards from the road. "They aren't what I would call a cabin."

Sarah laughed again. "These ain't cabins. These are soddies or sod huts. Come on and look mine over."

"Thank you," the sisters murmured. They looked to see that no move had been made to start to travel yet, so they smiled and followed Sarah to her home.

Rose and Alice and several of the other soldiers' wives walked over to see the soddies, too. They were invited to see some of the others as well. The owners explained that large bricks of sod had been cut where the prairie grass grew thick and laid on top of each other to create the walls. When they were high enough, logs had been laid over the top from front to back and more sod had been placed on top of the logs as roofing.

"Then sod bricks on top were packed together tightly to make it waterproof as possible," Sarah explained. "On mine the front wall is higher than the back to make the roof sloped so the rain runs off."

"That was a good idea," Katrin told her as they walked outside to see the roof. "Some of the soddies are shorter than the others. Can an adult stand up inside?"

"Oh, sure. Some have shorter walls, because they dug a square hole that was two or three feet deep into the ground first. That means they gotta step down into the house, but the owners claim that their soddy is warmer in the winter. I don't know if that's true. It's so blasted cold that it's hard to tell." She laughed at her own joke. "Some folks don't mind the cold inside. They have a separate room to sleep in. Not me," she said with a shake of her head. "I like to be warm when I sleep, so we all sleep spread out around the fire."

Katrin frowned and looked at Anna to find her doing the same. "There is no heat in the other room?"

"No, but it gets in there through the open door. The little ones still sleep by the fire in those soddies."

"I see that inside of each soddy, the floor is bare earth that has been packed hard from use. How can you clean the floor?" Anna asked.

"It just takes some sweeping, but when it gets broken up, I spread my wash water over it when I'm done with the clothes. It makes a nice hard surface." Sarah grinned. "Course, I can't do that in the winter. Wouldn't want to spend that long outside waiting for it to dry."

The homes were dark inside and lit only by the fire in the fireplace, because several had no windows at all and the rest only had one. Parchment paper or fabric had been stretched across a wooden frame set in the opening. The only natural light for the others came in through the door when it could be left open. "I'd rather have no light than the cold inside come wintertime," one housewife told them.

"That's why we fill in our window with sod blocks when it gets cold. Then in the spring we take them out," another of the soddy housewives said.

"I can't get used to the idea of living inside dirt walls. I can't imagine how such a home would ever feel clean," Anna admitted.

"I know what you mean. That's why we hung the big quilt my mother made on the wall. It covers the blocks and I like looking at it better than the sod blocks."

"We had a few boards left after my husband put up some shelves and made the table," Gertie told them. "We put them up to cover the wall behind the counter where I fix food so I don't have clumps of dirt falling into anything."

"Oh, dear. I hadn't thought of that happening," Katrin said.

"Oh, don't get us wrong. Soddies aren't bad. They're nice and tight except maybe around the door. They're a good sight warmer in the winter than a log cabin. Cutting the blocks is hard work though, but to build a cabin, a body's got to go into Minnesota and cut trees and then haul them back. That takes a while, but there's not much timber in Dakota Territory. A lot of what is here is bent over from growing in the wind, so we gotta go get straight ones."

"Here in Dakota Territory there is timber near rivers," another woman told them. "Now the government is encouraging homesteaders to plant trees on their land. You can prove up on a homestead grant just by planting trees now."

"We drove through trees each day coming from St. Paul. I can't help but wonder what it is going to be like to live on the prairie where there are few trees. What would that look like?" Katrin mused.

Sarah laughed. "Oh, I expect you get used to it. I guess we're lucky living near to the Red. We got trees to see."

"We have many new things to get used to," Anna said.

"But you'll come to love it. When you look up at the bright blue sky, you see that it seems to go on forever. At night you look up and see more stars than you can count. And if you drive into the prairie with the wind blowing on a sunny fall afternoon, you can see the tall golden grass dipping in waves just like golden waves on a big lake."

"I hope we come to love it like you do," Katrin said with a smile.

The cook rang the bell and the soldiers said it was time to leave. They thanked the women for the tour of their homes. "I hope we get a chance to see you again," Anna said.

"We get up to the fort when we can travel so maybe we'll see you there."

After all the thank you's and goodbyes had been said, the wagons moved on north.

Chapter 10

The wagon train didn't take long to reach the fort. A trumpet sounded and the stockade gates opened wide for them to enter. The soldiers there came out to greet them all as the wagons lined up inside with little room to spare. The soldiers riding in dismounted and tied their horses to the fence around the corral.

"I expected the fort would be bigger," Katrin said to the others in the coach as they waited for it to stop. "That log wall doesn't look high enough to keep anyone out."

"That lookout isn't much taller than the wall," Alice noted.

"But the land is pretty flat. Someone up there could see what's coming from a long way off," Rose put in.

"They saw us coming and blew the trumpet, didn't they, Eric? I know the soldiers will keep us safe inside," Anna said when she saw Eric frowning at the conversation. "We'll be perfectly fine here."

"Do you think they will let us stay here, at the fort, until we find where the Oleson brothers are living?" Katrin asked Anna.

"I don't know," Anna admitted. "Jake said the wagons are heading back to St. Paul tomorrow morning, so we can't stay in one of them."

The lieutenant put the sergeant in charge of getting the soldiers organized and into a line for inspection while the lieutenant went to check in with the colonel. The families climbed down from the wagons but stood by them while the soldiers talked to the soldiers already in the fort. The lieutenant returned with the fort's commanding officer, Colonel Albert Blake, and the new soldiers hurried into a line and stood at attention.

Everyone could see that standing at attention and looking smart in their uniforms was not a priority for this unit. After congratulating the men for successfully making the trek to the fort, the colonel said the new soldiers would have a couple of days rest to settle in. "Then we start patrols to find the pesky Indians and get them out of here," he announced with a sweep of his arm.

"The patrols should give my men a chance to learn the lay of the land, too," the lieutenant replied.

"Right. Just be aware there could be an Indian behind any tree with an arrow that he wants to put through your heart."

The two men walked together as the colonel reviewed the troops. They were a tired haggard-looking group, but they all saluted smartly. The colonel frowned at the gray parts of their uniforms and said they would do something about them.

"Welcome to Fort Abercrombie," he said to everyone when he had walked past them all. "My aide will show you single men where you can stow your things. We don't have a lot of room within the fort so those of you with families will be living in the soddies we're building about a half-mile west of here. Putting up more of them will be one of your first duties."

"The families won't be in the fort, sir?" the lieutenant asked.

"Yours will be in your quarters here, but the other families will be safe out there. It's so close that they can get into the fort right quick if there's trouble."

The colonel glanced at the fort's corral that was already full of horses. "The horses you've brought in for the men more than double the number we have here. They can stay in the corral for now where they can get to water and feed. The men will have to keep their saddles with them 'til we figure out how to store them." He shook his head. "We need more room for your men and for the horses by winter, and we need your men to build it."

"Yes, sir."

Colonel Blake turned to go back to his office. The lieutenant called out, "at ease, men," and followed the colonel. "Ah, sir, we have two women traveling with us who are here to find Ingor and Lars Oleson." The colonel stopped and turned back. "They said the brothers have been here a couple of years."

"Yes, yes, I'm new here, but I've heard of Ingor. He's a real maverick, and I think I heard he had a brother who settled down farther to the west, near the James River."

Adam frowned, wondering what the colonel had meant about one being a real maverick. He didn't like the idea of either sweet and gentle Anna or Katrin marrying such a man. "Will our patrol take us near their places? I'd like to meet them and tell them the women are here at the fort."

"We can arrange that. Always good for you to meet the local people. There are more every year now that the land has been opened for homesteading, and that means more people for us to protect."

"And the women, Miss Anna and Miss Katrin Anderssen? Can they stay here at the fort until we find the Oleson brothers?"

"I don't think there's room. We have to sort out the soddies for quarters for the officers' families. They may have to double up until we build some more, and they come first."

"Well, sir, for the time being, the sisters can have my quarters with my son, if they don't object to the arrangement. They've been taking care of him since my late wife's mother passed away on our journey here. I can bunk with the single men."

"Oh, I'm sorry to hear about your mother-in-law. Yes, yes, the women can stay there in your quarters with the boy for the time being. And when you find the Oleson brothers?"

"Their uncle sent the Anderssen sisters to marry them, sir."

The colonel grinned. "Well, we haven't had a wedding here since I arrived last fall. Wait 'til my wife hears this. Anything else?"

"No, sir. Thank you, sir," the lieutenant said with a salute.

With an abrupt nod, the colonel went on to his office. The lieutenant walked back to his men when the colonel's aide stepped forward.

"Sir, your quarters are there," he said, pointing to one of several doors in a long wooden structure that continued beyond the colonel's office. "The single men's barracks are there at the end. The men can take any empty bunk. And I can ride out and show the families to where they will be staying."

The lieutenant thanked him and relayed the barracks information to his men. "You men with families, get back on the wagons. They'll take you and your goods to where you'll be staying. You should be able to unload your packs and trunks from the wagons in time to get back here for the evening meal. You can't be expected to provide for yourselves until you move in and get things sorted out."

The wagons with their goods, and the coaches and wagons the families had been riding in turned out of the line once the passengers were back inside. Exiting the fort, they followed the colonel's aide who rode ahead of them. They turned west toward a row of soddies. The few families already living in them came out to greet them and to help them move in.

The single men had gotten any additional packs before the wagons left. They headed to the barracks with them, their saddlebags, and their bedrolls. They stored their personal property beneath their cot or in any empty spaces in the narrow cabinets that had been built in a row along the wall.

As soon as he could, the lieutenant sought out Anna and Katrin. They had taken their bags out of their coach and were standing with Eric. Beside him was the small case that Elsie had had with her. Eric was watching the teams of horses turn and head out the gate with the soldiers' families.

"They're taking Grandmother's trunk. Will I get my things that are in it?" Eric asked his father when he saw him coming.

Adam smiled. "Don't worry. They'll be back and we'll get it then. All the trunks were lashed together so it was easier to leave it on the wagon for now."

"But, don't we get to live in one of the soddies, too?" Eric asked.

"No, I've been given a room here in the fort," he explained. "If Miss Anna and Miss Katrin don't mind, they can stay with you in my room. I will bunk with the single men until we find the Oleson brothers and decide what each of you will do."

"But what about you?" Anna asked. "You shouldn't have to give up your room."

"There's a cot in the barracks for me," he replied with a smile for her concerned look. "That's fine for the time being. You don't mind staying with Eric?"

"Not at all," the sisters chorused.

"We didn't know what we were going to do with nowhere to stay," Anna added. "Thank you for arranging this."

"You don't have to worry. The colonel said you could stay here until we find the Oleson brothers."

"I don't know how we would manage without all the help you have given us," Anna told him.

"You don't have to thank me again, Anna. I'm happy to help. Now I have to find a cot or a straw mattress for Eric. You can sleep on the floor then, all right?" He smiled down at his son who nodded his head in response.

"He may find it more fun than sleeping in a bed," Katrin guessed.

"I've never slept on the floor in a house before," Eric put in. "But I slept on the ground outside and I think it must be like that, only I won't get rained on."

Adam laughed. "Right. You won't get rained on unless the roof leaks, and I don't think it does."

Eric turned to watch the drivers un-harnessing the teams on the coaches and the cook's wagon that stayed in the fort. There were more horses in a small area than he had ever seen before.

Adam turned to talk just to the sisters. "I want you to know that the day after tomorrow, I'll be leading many of the new soldiers out on patrol to get to know the lay of the land near the fort. When I meet homesteaders, I'll ask about the Oleson brothers. If I find them or someone who knows them, I will get a message to them that their brides…that you are waiting for them at the fort."

Katrin started to object, but Anna laid her hand on her arm and said, "That's good of you to do that for us. I didn't know how we would locate them without your help."

Adam nodded. "I'll let you get settled. Do you need help with your bags?"

Anna and Katrin shook their heads.

Adam turned to Eric and said, "Can you bring your case, Eric? You're going to see the room you'll be staying in."

Eric picked up Elsie's case to show he could handle it. "I can carry it all by myself."

"I'll have the trunk moved into my quarters when the wagons return," Adam promised. "Now I'd better get the men settled in the barracks." He nodded with a smile and headed for the barracks.

"Can we go now?" Eric asked, his voice showing his impatience. "This is heavy."

"Sure. You lead the way. It's the one with the open door there. We'll be coming right behind you."

"Why didn't you let me tell Adam?" Katrin whispered to Anna when Eric was too far ahead to hear.

"He's going to get word to the Oleson brothers to come here, Katrin. We have to meet them, and then you can explain that you don't want to marry one of them."

"Oh, this is so hard. What if they are really counting on us being their wives? Everyone says there aren't enough women out here to go around. What are we going to do if they insist?"

They stopped just before entering Adam's room. "I will marry one of them," Anna said, holding her sister's gaze. "I promised I would and I intend to keep that promise."

Katrin looked down at her fingers that were white because she was gripping her bags so tightly. She shook her head and in a barely audible voice said, "I can't. I just can't."

"I thought the sergeant might have told the lieutenant about the two of you," Anna remarked. "He doesn't seem to know anything about your plans."

"No, Tavis said it would be better for us to talk to the Oleson brothers first before he said anything to make our engagement official." Katrin looked at the ground and toed a small hole in the dirt with her shoe.

Anna smiled. "Hmm. He agrees that we must talk to them first." Now, if they could work it out, Anna was certain that the sergeant would be a good husband for her sister. He was an honorable, as well as a very capable, man.

"You don't have to look so happy that he agrees with you. You both think I'm impetuous." She heaved a quick sigh. "And I guess I am, but I truly love Tavis, Anna. I truly do."

"I know, Katrin. We'll work it all out." Anna wished she just knew how.

Eric had had time to go into the room and to come back to find out why they were going so slowly. "It even has a fireplace," he said with excitement.

"That will come in handy to keep you and your father warm next winter," Anna said with a smile. Her lip trembled though. It was hard to smile when she thought about the future in which Adam would not be in her life.

When the wagons were unloaded at the soddies and returned to the fort, the lieutenant saw to it that Elsie's trunk was taken to his quarters. With all the wagons empty, the drivers unhitched the rest of the teams and confined them in a temporary, roped-off, corral inside the stockade for the night. Once the horses were confined, the men fed and watered them. They would be ready for the trip back to St. Paul the next morning.

* * * *

Standing at the one window in her living room, the colonel's wife watched the wagons come and then go. She watched as the soldiers headed for the barracks, and she noticed two women who didn't leave with the others. Wondering why they stayed in the fort, she intercepted her husband as he headed back for his office after reviewing the new troops.

"Those two women," she snapped. "Why are they going into the lieutenant's room? You told me he was a widower and you can't tell me they are his daughters."

"No, no, dear," he said, patting her arm to calm her. "The lieutenant said they have come to marry the Oleson brothers who are settled here."

"Are they mail-order brides? I didn't expect that we would have that sort of thing going on here at the fort."

"No, I didn't bother to get the details, but I suspect the women arranged to marry the brothers in Norway and have followed them here now to give them a chance to get established."

She grinned. "Then that's very different. Soon we will have two brides and two grooms. How delightful. We will have a double wedding. Why, I've never been to a double wedding. This is a perfect reason for a party. Yes, we haven't had a party since we got here last fall."

Before the colonel could stop her, she headed right for Anna and Katrin, who were sitting on the steps in front of the lieutenant's quarters. A young boy was drawing pictures in the dirt near them. The sisters rose when she approached and introduced herself.

"We're so happy to meet you," they said nearly in unison. They laughed at saying the same thing and then Anna introduced herself, Katrin, and Eric to her.

"The colonel told me why you're here and I think it is so romantic." She patted her chest with one hand. "Goodness, you have come all this way to Dakota Territory to find the men you are promised to marry. This is wonderful. We have to make plans for the double wedding. We'll have it as soon as the brothers arrive to be the grooms." She laughed.

"But..." Anna tried to say.

"We can't have a wedding without the grooms, can we? Now I've never seen a double wedding, but we'll make this one something special. Everyone will want to come. We'll have to have music and dancing. Oh, it will be like old times. The colonel and I used to have such lovely parties before we came out west. This is just what we need to brighten things up around here."

"But you can't have a double wedding," Katrin blurted out when the colonel's wife drew a long enough breath to give her a chance to continue.

Anna grasped her arm to quiet her. "She means we don't want you to go to all the trouble," Anna put in quickly. She didn't think letting anyone know of Katrin and Tavis's plans would help at this point, and she worried it might get Tavis in trouble.

"No, no, it's no trouble. It will be so much fun," she insisted. "We haven't had a party since we got here last fall. 'Course the winter is just too cold to expect people to travel to get to the fort. Yes, and the snow. It keeps falling and never goes away until spring." Her face brightened with a bigger smile. "Oh, I just remembered. The circuit preacher will be here next week." She clapped her hands together. "It's perfect. If the brothers aren't here by then, we'll just ask him to wait until they come into the fort. Oh, if they haven't seen you since they came here, they'll be so surprised. Now I must go begin the planning." She laughed as she clapped her hands together again and twirled around to walk rapidly to her quarters, leaving Anna and Katrin staring after her.

"She doesn't know how surprised they will be after we tell them we're not marrying them," Katrin whispered. "Oh, dear. I hope we don't get Adam in trouble. Backing out of her special wedding party may put him in a bad position."

"As long as we're hoping impossible hopes, let's hope the Oleson brothers don't show up, and we can have the double wedding with the men we want to marry in their absence," Anna put in. She shook her head. "That's an awful lot to hope for," the ever-practical side of her added.

She drew her lower lip into her mouth and bit down. Yes, that was just too much for them to hope for, but giving up all hope was just as hard.

* * * *

The rented wagon and coaches pulled out at first light to return to St. Paul. They had two passengers heading east, which was an unexpected bonus for them. A middle-aged couple that had come out the previous fall to homestead had decided not to stay. Though they had filed for their land, they could not cope with the cold, inhospitable winter. They came through Wahpeton soon after the wagon train left the day before.

"The folks at Wahpeton told us the wagons were going back so we came right up here. We want to go back to Illinois. That's where we settled before coming here. There's a farm that's for sale next to my sister's place," the husband told the colonel. "It's more civilized and there is help nearby when you need it."

"And it doesn't get so cold," his wife put in.

"We're sorry to see you go," the colonel said. "Hate to see any settlers leave." He assigned a couple of the soldiers to help the couple put their bags and the trunk in one of the covered wagons.

"We can ride out of the sun under the canvas, too, but with plenty of breeze to keep us cool," the husband told the driver when he chose where they wanted to ride.

When their goods were on board, the couple climbed up. The wife set out their folded blankets to make a softer seat to sit on. Her husband tied their trunk to the side so it wouldn't move on the rough road. They waved goodbye as the wagon train pulled out.

"I hope they will be happier in Illinois than they have been here," Anna said to her sister. They had come out to watch the wagons leave, but she couldn't help but think of Katrin and herself.

Katrin looked at her. "Will we want to leave after staying through one winter?"

"I hope not," Anna replied.

"No, we have no where to go."

"Katrin, I don't think Lars and Ingor would have let us come if they didn't find living here good." Having too much work to do kept them from thinking about it long.

The Army had previous arrangements with two women, a soldier's wife and her teenaged daughter, whom they hired to wash and mend the single men's uniforms and other clothes each week as long as the weather permitted. Soldiers lined up galvanized washtubs and filled them with water from the river that the women had been heating in cast iron pots over an open fire.

The new soldiers assigned to the fort were happy to have clean clothes to put on, after having worn the same clothes for months. The only washing many of them had had was in the heavy rain or splashing about in a lake.

When the laundry and mending was done, the women looked through the uniforms in storage at the fort to outfit the new soldiers who had less than a full uniform. They were not successful in putting together a new complete uniform for all the men, but they came up with parts so they could at least change their clothes when it was their day to have their uniform cleaned. Some would have to wait for a full uniform until more arrived from the east, where they were made.

After he had watched the wagon train leave the fort early that morning and the washday activity after that, Eric asked permission of Anna to go watch the soldiers tending the horses in the corral. "But, please do not climb up the rails. I don't want to worry about you falling."

"Yes, ma'am," Eric replied with little enthusiasm.

With the boy out of harm's way, Anna and Katrin spent their first morning at the fort washing their clothes and Eric's. The women washing the uniforms were happy for the company and let them use a tub of water that the soldiers kept filled.

After the clothes dried spread out in the sun, the sisters brought chairs from the lieutenant's room out in front of the doorway and sat there in the sunlight to repair any garment that needed it.

"I've never seen so much damage along the hems of our skirts," Anna said.

"We walked for a lot of miles. Do you think it was the long blades of grass that wore through the fabric?" Katrin asked. "I know they wore the color off the leather of my shoes on the sides."

"But I never dreamed that grass blades could act like thin knife blades."

"Well, they are both blades." The sisters laughed at her little joke.

"Now that we've got them clean, we have no choice than to take the hems up a little to hide the damage," Anna said. "And we'll have to sew the edges of the worn spots together."

"Do you think this is why the women's skirts in Wahpeton and here all look a little shorter?"

Anna nodded. "It makes sense not to have them touching the ground. If we're not walking through damaging grass, it's mud that we're sinking into." She looked up at the blue sky.

"Anna," Katrin said softly, dropping her sewing to her lap. "What are we going to do if the colonel's wife goes through with the party? I've heard her spreading the word to all the families. She's expecting us to be the two brides at her double wedding celebration."

Anna avoided looking at her, because she didn't have an answer. "The soldiers don't leave to patrol between here and the James River until tomorrow. They'll be gone a week or maybe a little longer, I think. If they contact the Oleson brothers, it will be a while until they could arrive here."

"Yes, that's what Tavis said. Um, he's not going on the patrol," Katrin put in.

Anna's gaze jumped to meet her sister's. "What do you mean, he's not going? Doesn't the lieutenant want his Sergeant with him?"

"Tavis said the colonel wants someone who knows the land to go with Adam. He wants Tavis to be in charge of getting more cabins built west of the fort for the families so they'll be done long before winter hits. The families with one or no children had to double up in the soddies because there weren't enough."

"Well, that's good. Now that I think on it, it will be good for Adam and his men to have an experienced guide with them, a man who knows the land," Anna said, smiling and feeling better about it. "He can show them where to go and point out what they need to know. He should know better than anyone how to look out for Indians."

"I hope so," Katrin said.

The sisters sewed until they finished their hems. Then there were the holes in their stockings and Eric's plus the tears in the knee of his pants and the sleeve of one of his shirts. After carefully putting away their needles and thread, they went to find Eric.

Chapter 11

Eric and Jimmy, who had come into the fort to play with him while his parents worked at unpacking, were still watching the horses in the corral. Their fascination seemed endless. The sisters arrived at the corral just when the soldiers had sorted out the ill-fitting saddles and provided each soldier with a properly saddled mount. The sergeant ordered them into a two-man wide formation and announced they were going outside the fort to drill in the field where there was more room.

"They're going outside the fort. Can I go watch them there?" Eric asked Anna.

Anna looked around the stockade and suddenly smiled. "I've got a better idea. I know where you will have the best view and not miss a thing." She pointed to the lookout. "Let's go see if you can watch from up there."

Eric and Jimmy eagerly ran ahead to the wooden steps up to the lookout. "You go on up and ask the guard if you can watch from there," Anna called.

The boys scrambled up the steps and appeared back at the door moments later. "He said he shouldn't let us, but he will this once." Anna chuckled. "So can we stay up here?"

"If the guard says so, then you may, but don't you go bothering him. He's supposed to be watching for Indians," Anna insisted.

"We can help." He turned, but stopped and looked back at Anna. "Oh, and you were right. We can see all the men and their horses from up here."

"Good, because I don't want you going outside the fort."

"Yes, ma'am," Eric replied too quickly to sound like he meant it before he disappeared beyond the door.

The new men were sent out with those already stationed there. They drilled by riding in formation of two lines. They practiced keeping their horses even with the man's beside them, but for some who were not good horsemen, it took all their concentration. They knew the importance of staying with it until they could take their horse for granted and devote all their attention to searching the land around them for movement. They couldn't be concentrating on what their horse was doing when they should be watching for any Indians who might be nearby.

On the second round of drills after the noon meal, the colonel rode out to check on them. He selected ten of the best riders to go out on the first patrol the next day with Lieutenant Johnson and Sergeant Tom Stanton. The chosen men were from the new company and from among those who had been at the fort at least a year.

"I'm sending an experienced sergeant with you. Tom knows the territory. You'll soon pick out the landmarks so you'll know your way around. There's plenty of time for your sergeant to ride out then, too," the colonel told Adam. "We haven't heard of trouble this far to the east, but it's imperative that you keep an eye out. We can't afford to lose a single man."

"Yes, sir," the lieutenant said as he saluted and then ordered the men to take their mounts into the fort. "Give them a good brushing and check their hooves," he ordered. "Those of you going with me and Sergeant Stanton: we leave at first light tomorrow."

The lieutenant and the colonel led the soldiers riding in formation back into the open gates of the fort. Adam took care of his own horse while the aide took care of the colonel's. As soon as his horse was brushed and fed, he headed toward his quarters where the sisters were staying with Eric. He stopped at the well on the way and did the best he could to clean his face and hands. He wished he could strip off the wool uniform and bathe. Wearing wool in the summer was hot, but he knew he would appreciate the warmth when the fall and winter came to the northern plains.

Arriving at the room to which he had been assigned, he knocked. He heard Eric inside rushing to open the door. He hugged his son and swung him up into the air.

"We watched the horses in the corral and then we climbed up to the outlook and watched you and the soldiers ride their horses in lines. Miss Anna went with me, but not until they finished all the lady stuff they had to do, like washing clothes and sewing things. She even sewed the sleeve I ripped on my shirt."

Adam laughed. "So you're being good and not being a bother for these nice ladies?"

"Yes, Father. But since the soldiers brought in Grandma's trunk yesterday, Anna made me find clean clothes to put on today. And she made me take a bath first," he grumbled. "She isn't going to make me do that very often, is she?"

Adam laughed again. "I imagine she will make that demand as often as it is necessary."

"If you like to spend time alone with your son, Lieutenant," Anna said smiling at their conversation, "we can go for a walk."

The bell rang to announce that supper was ready before he could answer.

"Oh, good," Eric said, grabbing his father's hand and pulling him toward the door. "Let's go eat. I'm hungry."

"Ladies first, Eric," Adam prompted.

The two of them waited and held the door while the sisters filed out. When Anna passed, he laid his hand on her arm to stop her.

"After supper, may I speak with you?"

"Of course," she said before going on out.

Having no appetite because she was worried about what Adam wanted to tell her, Anna made herself eat anyway. Now that food was made available to her, it would have been foolish not to eat it. However, she couldn't say what she had eaten even just minutes after the meal.

The meal was pleasant in that they caught up on the news from Rose and Alice. They told them all about the soddy they were sharing and the one they would build for Rose to move into. They were going to build a larger one for her and Jethro, because she was going to have another child.

Anna had a hard time paying attention to all that everyone was saying. She was thinking about talking with Adam after the dinner was over. Tonight might be her last chance to talk to him before the Oleson brothers showed up to claim their brides. Tears burned in her eyes at the thought. When she wiped away one that escaped, she had to make an excuse that she might have gotten something in her eye. The others thought nothing of it and went on talking about the soddies.

Leaving the hall with Eric after helping clear the tables, Katrin said, "After you say good night to your father, I'll read you a story from one of your Grandmother's books before you have to go to bed. Would you like that?"

Eric jumped at the chance and ran to his father who was walking beside Anna. Facing his father, he walked backwards ahead of him to say good night and tell him Katrin was going to read to him.

Stopping him, Adam knelt down and held his shoulders. "You remember that I'm going out on patrol at dawn tomorrow."

Eric nodded. "I know. Will you see many Indians?"

"I don't know, but frankly, I hope not. I'd like my men to be less green before that happens."

Eric laughed. "Your men would look funny if they were green."

"Yes, you're right. Listen, while I'm gone I want you to watch out for Miss Anna and Miss Katrin, and you mind what they tell you to do."

"Yes, sir." His face brightened. "Sergeant McDougal said he would let me ride on his horse each day if I was good."

Adam laughed. "That's mighty nice of him. Be sure to follow his orders." Eric nodded. "Now give me a hug and unless you're getting up before dawn to see us off, I'll see you in a week or ten days."

Eric eagerly wrapped his arms around Adam's neck and gave him the hug he asked for. "Maybe I'll be able to ride a horse all by myself by the time you get back," he said, hopefully.

"I think that will happen when your legs are long enough to reach the stirrups," Adam replied with a smile.

"Oh, yes. I didn't think of that."

"But in the meantime, you have fun riding on Sergeant McDougal's horse."

A broad grin grew on Eric's face. "I will. Good night then."

Unable to resist, Adam gave him another quick hug and watched him walk into his quarters with Katrin before he rose. He turned to Anna and reached for her hand.

"Walk with me for a while?"

She nodded. He kept hold of her hand.

"I've missed being with Eric for most of his life. I'm glad to have the chance now to see him more often. I feel like I have a lot of catching up to do."

"He's a good boy and will become a man you can be proud of."

He smiled. "Yes, Elsie did a good job raising him. I don't know what I would have done without her."

"I was so sorry she didn't make it all the way here to live with you."

He stopped walking. "Frankly, I think she knew that she could never complete the journey. She wasn't well before we left New York."

"Then why would she come? She must have had friends back East. She could have stayed there."

"Yes," Adam replied. "I just think she wanted to be with her family."

"Yes, with family around her, she didn't have to die alone."

"Exactly."

They took a few steps in silence.

"Her trunk is full of wonderful things for Eric," Anna told him. "She packed toys, a slate and chalk, plain paper, and pencils, too. There are clothes that are too big for him now, but I'm sure he'll grow into them soon. Oh, and the books. There were so many books."

"That must be why it weighed so much."

"She thought a lot about what a boy out here would need and want to have."

Smiling, he tucked her hand into his bent arm as they walked to a shadowed spot on the far side of the stockade where no one would hear their conversation or see them. Once hidden, conversation wasn't sufficient. He pulled her into his arms and kissed her. Clinging to each other for the last time, their actions spoke the words that they could not say.

They didn't dare stay there more than a few minutes. Adam would take no chances at ruining her reputation.

Concerned about leaving her and Katrin at the fort with his son to watch, he asked, "You're sure you'll be all right here with Eric?"

Anna smiled. "Yes, Adam. We'll be fine. He loves watching the men training or caring for the horses."

"And he can help you unpack what you need for him from Elsie's trunk."

"Oh, yes, and there are so many other things in there that you won't need here in the fort. She packed dishes and even cooking pots. But Eric loves having so many books the best. Katrin and I are taking turns reading to him at night before he goes to sleep."

"You make it so easy for me not to worry a moment about him."

"That's the way it should be. You just need to take care of yourself so nothing happens to you. We want you to come back to us."

"This patrol is going just as far as the James River. Sergeant Stanton says it's about a hundred miles into the Territory, but it's a start at my learning my way around."

"Am I being silly to ask you to be careful out there?"

He smiled broadly. "We should all be safe and return with no problems. Ah, I have to say it, Anna. If I find the Oleson brothers, I will ask them to come to the fort right away."

"Yes, of course," Anna said, looking down at her hands knotted at her waist. "There's no sense putting it off. It will just make it harder on everyone."

He stepped closer again and took her hands and held them in his. "Anna, if you ever need help or anything, even after you are married, you can come to me."

"Thank you, Adam. I shall always remember you and all you have done for us."

"And, well, if the colonel's wife has her way and plans a double wedding, I…I want you to know that I will not be in attendance. I couldn't bear to watch you wed another man when I want you to be my wife."

"Oh, Adam," she managed before throwing her arms around his neck and sobbing.

He held her until her tears no longer fell. "I love you, Anna. I always will."

"And I love you."

One last kiss acknowledging their love for each other was all they had time for before he walked her back to his quarters and closed the door after she went in.

He tried to wish that he would never find the Oleson brothers. But he couldn't wish that. His conscience wouldn't let him.

* * * *

The rising sun painted the sky pale gray on its way to a brilliant royal blue as the soldiers rode out of Fort Abercrombie the next morning. Anna had intended to get up and dress in time to see them off, but she hadn't been able to sleep much during the night. When she finally did get to sleep, she only awoke when she heard activity outside their room. She had no time to get dressed and go outside to see them off. They were leaving already.

Upset with herself, she opened the door just an inch or two and watched the men mount up and form a double line. Still in her long cotton nightgown, she couldn't step out to watch. As the columns passed her door, Adam looked in her direction. She saw a small smile brighten his face.

She kissed her fingers and blew it toward him, hoping none of the other men noticed. "Come home to me," she whispered, even though she knew he couldn't hear her.

When the soldiers were out of sight of her doorway, she closed the wooden door and leaned her head against it. She stayed there until she could no longer hear the horses and the order had been shouted to close the gate. Returning to bed, she crawled in and managed another hour of sleep on a damp pillow.

The sisters and Eric rose at a normal time for the fort activity and fell into a pattern of activities while the patrol was gone. Watching the horses and watching the men drill was a must for Eric. A couple of afternoons, they walked the half-mile to go visit Rose and Alice. While Anna and Katrin chatted with them, Eric and Jimmy watched the soldiers building more soddies.

"I like watching the big horses pull the sod plow," he explained. "That cuts the soil just the right size for the blocks. Then the soldiers just have to cut the block shape and it's ready to put in a wall."

One day when the soldiers were cutting grass to put in a mound to have to feed the horses, Eric wanted to help. Anna was glad the soldiers backed her up in saying he was too young to handle a scythe. Visions of Eric with a cut leg were too vivid in her imagination to even think of allowing him to do it. He had to be content carrying armfuls of cut grass to throw on a mound. He and Jimmy got sidetracked a little when they threw the grass at each other, but the soldiers didn't seem to mind. The boys were having fun and a few strokes of their wooden-tined rake got up all the scattered grass.

On the days they stayed within the fort, Eric spent most of his time watching the horses. Meanwhile, the colonel's wife gave the sisters no time free of thinking about the upcoming wedding. She planned and plotted and soon the whole fort and the soddies to the west were buzzing with talk of their double wedding.

"Dresses!" she said on one visit to the lieutenant's room where the sisters sat reading to pass the time. "What will you wear?" she wanted to know.

"We brought dresses from Norway to wear," Anna told her. "You needn't worry yourself."

"You brought dresses. Yes, that was wise. How many do we have to choose from?"

"Choose? We each have one. They're the only fancy dresses we have," Katrin added.

"Hmm," she said with a frown. "Well, let me see them," she insisted.

The sisters pulled their fancy dresses from their bags and laid them on the bed.

"Oh, dear," the colonel's wife said, the frown deepening in her brow.

"Is something wrong with the dresses?" Anna asked. "Is this not what a bride would wear for her wedding here?"

"Oh, I suppose they are fine, but they are very crushed from being in your cloth bag."

"The bags were often used as a pillow or pad to make a hard bench softer," Anna told her, smiling at the memories.

"Oh, dear."

"We thought we would worry about getting the wrinkles out when we got closer to the wedding," Katrin explained.

"Closer? My goodness, we might just be a few days now from the big day. No telling how quickly the patrol will return to the fort."

"But I don't expect the Oleson brothers to return with them. They'll come as soon as they can after they get the message that we're here."

"The men will find the grooms. I just know they will. And the lieutenant seems to be very persuasive. He'll bring them back on the double."

Anna and Katrin looked at each other with identical frowns.

"You must hang these dresses out and we'll see tomorrow what is to be done about making them more presentable. Heating an iron to the right temperature is so unpredictable. Maybe the cook could boil a big pot of water and we could hang the dresses over it. I've heard that steam helps make wrinkles disappear."

She paused in her rapid-fire speech a moment longer to study the dresses. "Oh, dear, the cook. I almost forgot. I must go speak to the cook. I tried to tell him about the food I wanted to serve, but he keeps telling me that he knows nothing of making the sweet delights we had in New York. But don't you worry. I copied my recipes for him so the party will be perfect."

She walked toward the door and turned for one more look at the dresses still on the bed. "Yes, we'll do something about the dresses," she promised before she swept out the door to go find the cook.

The sisters looked at each other and then at the dresses. Katrin lifted the sleeve of her dress and gently rubbed her thumb over the fabric. "I always liked this dress. I would be happy to be married in it."

"And so you shall be," Anna insisted.

"You don't think the wrinkles will be too bad?"

"We cannot let the opinion of others change our minds, and besides, these are the only fancy dresses that we have. Wishing for a change is useless."

Katrin looked at her sister and smiled. "Yes, and we should be thinking more of changing the groom than what we are to wear, but I'm counting on a change there."

Anna sighed but said no more about the grooms. "Come on. We can hang up these dresses to see what wrinkles will disappear," Anna said as she lifted her dress and hung one shoulder over a hook imbedded in the wall beside the dresser.

Katrin took her dress and did the same on the hook the other side of the dresser.

"Now they look like curtains hanging beside an open window, only there's no window there," Anna said with a laugh.

Katrin laughed, too. "I don't want to think of the weddings now. Let's go see what mischief Eric has gotten into."

"Yes, but you can't fool me. Tavis was giving him a ride and you just want to see Tavis."

"Is that very terrible of me?"

"I'm not the one to judge you," Anna told her. "Let's wait until the Oleson brothers come for that."

* * * *

Instead of heading north along the packed road by the river, the soldiers on patrol had headed straight west. Each soldier rode his horse, and several had the reins of a packhorse tied to his saddle. That horse carried their provisions for the week including venison jerky and the makings for flapjacks that could be fried over a small fire in their cast iron skillet.

The soldiers' families living in the soddies a half-mile out waved as they passed and wished them well. Riding through the flat and wide Red River valley was easy. The sun was shining brightly with few clouds to mar the brilliant blue sky.

They found a road that had been packed by wagons and horses and stayed on that for a time. It cut through tall grass and a few shrubs. The landscape was very different from Minnesota.

"Not many places for an Indian to hide here," the lieutenant said to Sergeant Marks who rode at his side.

"The grass is high enough to hide them if they're on foot and bend over, but we would see their horses. I think we'll be all right in the grass, but when we near trees, we have to keep a sharp lookout."

They rode for a couple hours before they saw smoke coming from the chimney of a soddy well off the road. The fields around it had been plowed and a crop of some kind of grain was a few inches high.

"We'll stop here, Sergeant. I want to ask about the Oleson brothers every chance we get."

Each time they stopped at a homesteader's soddy, Lieutenant Johnson was introduced by the Sergeant who seemed to know everyone. The lieutenant then asked about any Indian activity in the area. All the homesteaders said they had no trouble although a couple of old Indians had come their way begging for food that spring.

"They scared the children," the wife complained.

"We gave them enough to get them to move on. We ain't seen them since," the husband said.

"And we don't want to," the wife added.

The soldiers accepted invitations to fill their canteens and then they rode on.

The soldiers slept on their bedrolls on the ground at night. They took turns on watch, but saw and heard no sounds made by two legged animals.

As they neared the James River on the third day of their patrol, one homesteader told them he'd heard of a renegade band that attacked a family to the northeast. The lieutenant promised to swing up that way the next day after stopping at the nearby homesteads.

"Lars Oleson lives about two miles from here," one homesteader told him. "Go to the abandoned homestead and turn south. It's only a mile more."

The lieutenant thanked him and the men took off in that direction. But what would he find, he wondered. Would Lars Oleson have a soddy built and fields plowed and a crop growing in preparation for his bride's arrival?

They passed the empty soddy and noticed the kitchen garden that had been overgrown with grass and weeds. The house was good sized and Adam couldn't help but wonder why the residents had left there. He knew the winters were harsh, but he would have to ask Oleson when they met. He didn't like to think that Anna or Katrin would be suffering so greatly that they would wish to leave. He took a deep breath and tried to concentrate on memorizing the landmarks around them.

In no time they approached a wide sod house and saw two men and a woman working in a fenced garden near the house. Nearby, a small child played with a few wooden toys. Riding closer, he could see that the house was larger than others he'd seen. It was built of sod, but the end where a regular man-size door stood open was attached to another taller sod structure with a taller and wider door that also stood open. Dismounting, he saw two horses in stalls inside that end of the structure.

He handed his reins to the sergeant and told him to order the soldiers to dismount and wait. He walked toward the garden as the occupants came out of the makeshift gate to meet him. Then he noticed the rifles leaning beside the gate not far from the gardeners.

"I'm looking for one of the Oleson brothers," Adam said without hesitation.

The tall blond man said, "That's me."

"I'm Lieutenant Adam Johnson, new to Fort Abercrombie."

"Good to know you," he said, offering his hand to shake. "I am Lars Oleson and this is my wife Lissa. That's her brother Wally." He ruffed the child's hair and added, "And this is my son, Berg."

Adam could not stifle the grin that took over his face. He coughed into his gloved hand to hide it. "Ah, we bring you news that, from what you've said, you may not want to hear."

"News?" the other man, who Adam could see was probably only sixteen or eighteen years old, asked. "Who do we know that would send us news with the Army?"

Feeling them all looking at him, Adam cleared his throat. "The news is that Anna and Katrin Anderssen have arrived at the Fort, and they are looking for you and your brother. They were sent here by your uncle to be your wives."

Chapter 12

Adam watched as Lars frowned, his wife gasped, and the young man slapped his thigh and began to laugh.

"I don't think they'll let you have two wives out here," Wally said, still laughing.

"They're at the fort now?" Lars asked, his brow furrowed in a frown.

Adam nodded. "We're going to circle north and go back past your brother's place to tell him and then head for the fort. Can you go to talk to the sisters as soon as you can get ready? You obviously aren't going to marry one of them, but you need to tell them that to their faces. They've come a long way. It's the least you can do."

"You're right," Lars said.

"Your uncle must not have gotten your letter saying that we were married. What will the sisters do now?" Lissa asked. "Where will they live?"

"They cannot decide what they will do until they learn what they are not going to do," Adam put in carefully. "Can you come to the fort now?"

"We'll pack up, and we can leave first thing tomorrow. Tell my brother we'll meet him there."

Adam agreed. "Before we ride on, have you heard of any trouble in these parts with renegade parties of Indians?"

Lars shook his head. "Not here, but there's trouble to the north. Some Indians escaped the Army and ran to Canada. A few come down to hit a place and then they retreat north, where they feel safe. They seem to do as much damage here as they can, steal food, and money if they find it, and then run."

Adam nodded and swung into his saddle.

"Thank you for stopping here."

"Is your brother's cabin all the way back to the Red River?"

"No," Lars told him. "You'll cross the James River and head to the south edge of the trees on the Sheyenne River. Follow that to where it starts south and you can't miss his cabin. It's a ways before you come to the Red River."

"You know where that is?" Adam asked Sergeant Stanton.

"Yes. It should be easy to find," the Sergeant told him.

"My brother had some complaints about attacks in that direction, but that was last summer. I haven't heard anything since then," Lars told him.

After the men had filled their canteens with the clean, cold well water at the homestead, Adam led his patrol to the north. He had more homesteads to check on before they stopped for the night. The sergeant was correct about the location of all the settlements in the area.

"I sure am glad to see you on patrol," one homesteader told them as he came out of his soddy with a shotgun in his hand. "A man has a right to feel safe in his own home, and when we hear news of an uprising, we sure don't." His wife and child watched them from the doorway but didn't step outside.

"You've heard of recent trouble?" the lieutenant asked him.

"Man came through here yesterday and he was moving fast. He said he saw a dozen or so Indians camping farther north—north of the Sheyenne. Soon as he saw them, he took off south. He'd wanted to homestead around there, but he wasn't going to stay in that area until them Indians is cleared out. Can't say I blame him."

"We're heading that way," the lieutenant told him. "We'll check it out."

"You keep your eyes open. They have a way of showing up where you don't expect them."

"Thanks. We'll do that."

He signaled the men to mount up and they took off heading north again. They crossed the Sheyenne River, stopping to water and rest the horses. They continued on north where one homesteader said there had been an Indian raid. It didn't take long before they began to smell the smoke.

"That's got to be smoke I smell and it's been getting stronger, but I can't see any rising," the sergeant said, standing in his stirrups and looking around.

"Let's find out what it is. Seems to be coming from that way," the lieutenant said, pointing north. "Keep your eyes open, men," the lieutenant called over his shoulder.

"The farther north we go, the stronger it gets," the sergeant said.

It didn't take them long to find the source of the smoky odor. A small burned-out cabin that appeared only big enough to have one room was now a skeleton of charred boards. A few rocks stood on top of each other where the fireplace must have been. Built near to trees along a creek, the homesteader had constructed a log cabin from the trees rather than sod blocks.

"I think a trapper and his wife lived out here. Not much of a talker. They liked to stay to themselves," the sergeant said.

The lieutenant pointed to two rectangular rock mounds that sat several yards from where the cabin had been. "Looks like whoever told the other settlers about the attack had found them and buried them."

The sergeant nodded.

Adam ordered his men to see if they could find any hints as to what happened. It didn't take long for his men to find arrows and one spear that had hit a tree and splintered.

"If the people in the cabin ran out to escape the fire, they were killed," the sergeant put in. "I hope it was quick."

The lieutenant nodded. "Nothing more we can do now. Let's get away from the smell and find a place to camp for the night farther east. At first light we'll go find the other Oleson brother's cabin and then head back to the fort with him from there to tell the colonel what we found." He assigned the men to take turns on watch during the night. The cabin hadn't been burned all that long ago, and he wasn't taking any chances on being surprised. Once ready to start out in the morning, he urged his men to be on the lookout for movement.

They stopped at another homestead and heard the same news. He'd been the one who found the burning cabin and the dead trapper and his wife.

"There wasn't much of 'em left and nothing more I could do but bury them," the man told the lieutenant.

"Seen any Indians since then?"

"No, I ain't seen any Indians since then, and I don't want to," he snapped. "Just clear them out. This is our land now, and they should be chased out."

The lieutenant thanked him without comment, and he and his men moved on east. They spotted a curl of smoke rising and moving with the breeze by late morning. In the distance they could see the Sheyenne turning to the south. This had to be the other Oleson brother's place.

As they rode closer, they saw an Indian woman dressed in a leather tunic with fringe over leather pants with leather moccasins. She held a rifle aimed at them. The soldiers all pulled their rifles out and aimed them at her.

"Hold your fire," the lieutenant shouted.

The woman lowered her rifle slowly from her shoulder, but kept it aimed at them. The lieutenant reined his horse to ride closer to her. His own weapons were holstered.

"I thank you for not shooting my wife," a male voice said from the woods behind her.

Surprised, the lieutenant turned to see a man with blond hair and beard, also with a rifle aimed right at him. "*Got im himmel*," the lieutenant swore in Norwegian without thinking. "Does everyone want to kill us?"

Hearing the Norwegian, the man lowered his rifle and laughed. "You speak my mother tongue. You have come a long way to dress in blue out here."

The lieutenant relaxed his body. "Your name wouldn't be Ingor Oleson, would it?"

The man walked toward the Indian. "Yes, it is," he said. Reaching her, he said, "This is my wife, Still Water, and yes, it's all legal like in the white man's way." He walked around behind her and looked at something on her back. "This little papoose is my son. And who might you be?"

Both the Oleson brothers were married. Taking his rifle with him, Adam slid out of his saddle and handed the reins to the sergeant who called out to tell the men to dismount. Walking toward Ingor, he introduced himself. "I'm glad to make your acquaintance," he said as he shook his hand. "Ma'am," he said with a touch to the brim of his hat, looking at Still Water. He was glad to have the few moments to recover from the shock of realizing that both Oleson brothers had broken their promise. Anna was now free from her promise. She could be his wife. "I just arrived with my men from New York. Now that the war's over, they are moving soldiers out here to strengthen the forts."

"What are you doing out here near where we live? I thought the trouble was to the northwest of us," Ingor put in.

"There was trouble out that way. We found a burned out small one-room cabin and two graves. You know anything about that?"

The bearded man glanced at his wife and tugged on his beard. "Sounds like a trapper I met who lived out that way with his wife. They had a small place and didn't like folks stopping by."

"Signs were that it was Indians," Adam told him with a glance at his wife whose expression never changed.

"Signs?" Ingor asked.

Adam turned back to the sergeant. "Show them the arrows," he ordered.

The sergeant pulled them free of the rope around his bedroll and held them up. Ingor's wife muttered something, but Adam didn't understand it. Her gaze locked with her husband's for a few seconds, and she went back to picking up kindling.

"They're Sioux," Ingor said. He sighed heavily. "They come down and raid here and there and then go back north. The rest of the tribe stays peacefully in Canada, where they feel safe. They don't approve of what this renegade band does."

"That's what we've heard. I guess we need to be at the right place at the right time to catch the few that come down here on raiding parties."

Ingor nodded. "It won't be easy. Their leader moves quicker than the wind. Other soldiers have tried to find him and failed."

"He got a name?"

"Tall Cloud. Tried to kill me once, but she talked him out of it," he replied with a jerk of his head toward his wife. "I always thought he might try again, but we haven't seen him since last summer."

"And that is good," Still Water said, arranging the wood in her arm so she wouldn't drop any of it. Ingor stepped over to her to help with one that stuck out far enough to catch on trees she passed.

"But what are you doing here now, Lieutenant? You don't have enough men with you to be hunting for Indians."

"No, I'm getting to know the territory, and I'm looking for you. I have a message for you."

Ingor stepped closer. His beard hid his mouth, but Adam could see the frown on his brow. "What message? Something happen to my brother?"

Adam shook his head. "No. I have a message from the women your uncle sent from Norway to be your bride and your brother's. They are sisters—Anna and Katrin Anderssen. They are at Fort Abercrombie right now awaiting your arrival." Adam's grin grew as he passed on the news.

Now it was Ingor's turn to swear. He looked at his wife and then at Adam. "I thought my brother was sending our uncle a letter to say we were both married. I didn't expect brides to show up here." He sighed. "I think you'd better tell us all about it, and you can tell us why you seem so happy about it, too. Come over to the cabin. There's a water trough there for your horses, and we got some coffee."

Waiting for Ingor and his wife to start out ahead of him, Adam got a better view of the baby that Still Water carried strapped on her back as she turned and walked back to the cabin ahead of them with the wood she had gathered since their arrival. He could only see the child's face, but he appeared to be asleep and never fussed a bit.

"I told your brother the news yesterday, and he said he will meet you at the fort to talk to the sisters. You really need go to the fort now, too. You owe those sisters an explanation."

"Yes, and it won't be easy. They came expecting husbands and end up with nothing."

"Might be easier on them than you suspect," Adam said. "But I'll let them tell you why."

"Give us a few minutes to pack some things and saddle a horse."

Adam nodded. As Ingor leaned over to retrieve his own rifle that he had leaned against a tree, Adam turned back to tell his men they would be leaving for the fort after watering the horses. He heard an unusual sound like the wind in a narrow passage. He didn't get a word out before an arrow pierced his back. Bent over by the force of the hit, he looked down at the other end of the arrow protruding from the center of his chest, not believing what he saw. Ingor grabbed him before he fell and sat him down with his side against a tree.

"Indians!" the sergeant shouted. "Get down!"

By then several Indians had appeared from the woods, and the soldiers fired at will to stop them. Ingor shot one and took the lieutenant's rifle for another shot. Still Water, using the corner of the stable as cover, raised her rifle. One Indian on horseback at the back of the group shouted as his men fell before him. He raised his arm holding a spear as he urged his horse toward Ingor. Ingor raised the lieutenant's rifle and shot him square in the chest. With a grunt he dropped the spear and fell backwards off his horse. Only two Indians remained. Seeing their leader fall, they reversed direction and fled. The soldiers shot at them but couldn't tell if they had hit them. Neither fell from his horse as they disappeared into the woods.

Adam's chest burned and suddenly he had little strength. The sergeant knelt at his side. "They got two of our men," he reported, "counting you. We got all but two of them."

Still Water ran to the lieutenant's side. As soon as she saw what had happened, she ran back to the cabin. "I get bandages," she called back to them.

Ingor squatted next to the lieutenant. "Hold his shoulders," Ingor ordered.

"What are you going to do?" the sergeant demanded to know.

"I'm going to try to save his life," Ingor told him gruffly.

The sergeant held the lieutenant as Ingor took hold of the arrow with both hands and broke off the point. Adam tried to muffle his cry of pain as it shot through him. His head fell back against the tree. Ingor pulled a splinter loose from the broken end of the arrow and stepped around to kneel behind him. Bracing his hand against Adam's back, he pulled the arrow out. Unable to stop it, Adam cried out in pain this time.

"Take his jacket off," Ingor told the sergeant who did it with one of the other soldier's help. "The shirt, too."

Blood flowed down his chest and his back. Still Water returned and folded the cloth pieces she had brought. She laid one on each open wound with some white powder on each one. "Push on these. We cut shirt to make strip long enough to tie around chest and hold these in place."

"We got to get him to the fort," the sergeant insisted. He turned back to talk to one of the men who had come to report on the other soldier who had been shot with an arrow.

"He took an arrow through the arm. We took it out like he did for the lieutenant, and I don't think it damaged the bone. It ain't bleeding anything like the lieutenant's. We wrapped it up good."

"We did all right then if only two were hit," the sergeant assumed out loud.

"He aimed at me and your lieutenant took the arrow," Ingor said with a glance at his wife. "I knew he'd come back. But he won't bother us again thanks to your rifle, Lieutenant. Mine's a single shot, so I took yours to shoot him."

"They took us by surprise," the sergeant said. "We outnumbered them, but why didn't they get more of us?"

"Judging by all the arrows in the tree behind your lieutenant, I'd say they had orders to get me first."

"They weren't shooting at the other men who were shooting at them," the other soldier helping noted.

"It was time for them to die," Still Water put in. She took the strip that she had cut from the lieutenant's shirt and, with the help of the sergeant, wrapped it around his chest to hold the pads in place. "I tie tight. It will be hard to breathe, but must stop bleeding."

"If your men can pull over the wagon that's by the barn, we can make a bed of dried grass from the pile by the barn to make your injured men comfortable before we harness up the horses. We leave now and we can get to fort tonight. Road along the Red River is easy to follow in the dark," Ingor said.

The men followed his directions and threw grass from Ingor's barn store in the back. They pulled it to the tree where the lieutenant still sat leaning against the tree. The sergeant took the blanket from the lieutenant's bedroll and spread it out over the straw and then four men lifted him into it. The other injured soldier climbed in with their help and lay down beside him.

Meanwhile the other soldiers rounded up all their horses and three that remained behind that the Indians had been riding. Ingor finished harnessing his horse team to the wagon as Still Water came out of the cabin with sacks of food and other things they would need for the trip. She put them and skins of water under the driver's seat. One of the soldiers whose horse had been killed followed the sergeant's order to ride the lieutenant's horse. They tied Ingor's other horses and the Indians' mounts on the back of the wagon.

"I got to take them with us," Ingor said. "There's no one to take care of them if I leave them here."

"I fed baby so he can go until dark," Still Water said to Ingor. He smiled and squeezed her arm affectionately before he helped her up onto the seat.

"Sir? What about the Indian bodies?" one of the soldiers asked.

The sergeant looked in that direction and frowned. "I can see one of the fallen Indians is missing. He must not have been dead. They can take care of their own dead. We got to get out of here before they come back with more of their friends. Mount up, men."

Some of the men rode in front of the wagon and the rest behind it. Once they saw the Red River, they followed it south. While the men chewed on venison jerky for their supper, they stopped to rest and water the horses only when necessary. Still Water changed the bandages on the injured men and managed to nurse her infant child at the last stop. The men gave her all the privacy she needed and they were ready to continue the moment she was.

"Thank you, ma'am," the second injured one said when she had finished checking on his wounded arm. "When I signed on, they said I was coming out here to kill Indians. I never figured that one would be so kind as to help me and save our lives."

"I hope you remember that," she said softly. "We don't want to kill whites. We just want to keep our homes where we have lived for generations." The soldier had nothing to say to that.

The lieutenant passed in and out of consciousness as they rode south. "That is good. He not feel so much pain," Ingor told the worried sergeant.

The soldiers had all fought the War Between the States, but none of them had ever seen a man injured by an arrow. They didn't know if that was worse or better than having a bullet pass through. Except that when they thought about it, a bullet to the chest probably wouldn't have gone all the way through. Fishing out a bullet and the infection that would surely follow most likely would kill him as it had thousands of men during the war. Getting the arrow out though, they didn't know if the lieutenant would make it or not. They only knew the bleeding had to stop.

When they neared the fort, the sergeant sent a man ahead to alert the colonel. The gates were open and men were ready with stretchers. There was no doctor there, only a soldier who had been on medical duty during the war. He checked the wounds while the men were still in the wagon.

Civilians and soldiers crowded around the men when the wagon stopped on the parade ground. Anna looked over all the men arriving on horseback to find Adam and didn't. Her gaze jerked to the wagon and saw he was being moved onto a stretcher. She ran to the colonel and clutched his arm. "Your men can put him in his own bed. I'll take care of him."

Before his wife, standing close by, could say it wasn't proper, he gave the command to do so. The other wounded soldier was taken to the small room in the barracks set aside for the sick and wounded. The medical duty soldier followed the stretcher-bearers to see the lieutenant was cared for first. Another soldier followed to assist him. Sergeant McDougal went in, too, but not before he asked Anna to wait outside. In the room they undressed the lieutenant and put him to bed to check his wounds.

Ingor and Still Water, her child strapped on her back again, walked over to Anna just as Katrin ran to her side with Eric. Anna knelt down and stroked Eric's upper arms.

"Eric, your father has been injured. The soldiers are putting him to bed and seeing what they can do to help him."

"I want to see him," Eric insisted as he started past Anna toward the cabin.

"The medic is with him now," Anna said to stop him. She picked him up and held him in her arms as he began to cry. "We'll be able to see him as soon as they are done. We'll go in together."

He nodded and wiped his runny nose on his sleeve.

Having heard his native language, Ingor introduced himself and his wife and child.

Forgetting to even say they were pleased to meet him, Anna and Katrin stared at him. "You're married?" the sisters asked at once.

Ingor nodded and the sisters each smiled. "I don't know why that makes you smile, but the lieutenant liked to hear it, too."

"I'm sorry, but that's because I have picked the man I want to marry," Katrin told him before Anna could take a breath to speak. "I know I promised to marry you or your brother, but I just can't. Now I know I don't have to."

Ingor nodded. "Now I understand," he said as the medic and the two soldiers came out of the cabin. They all turned to hear what they had to say.

"Wound looks clean, but he's lost a lot of blood. It seems to be bleeding more now that we moved him, and that's not a good sign. Good thing you took the arrow out, but it may have nicked an artery that opened up again with the new movement."

"What can we do to stop the bleeding?" Anna asked. She was afraid she knew the answer already but had to ask. She felt light headed and set Eric on the ground without taking her eyes off the medic.

"Sorry, ma'am." He shook his head. "I don't know what more we could do. It doesn't look good. Just see that he doesn't move," he said before he walked on toward the barracks.

"Arrow?" Eric called out. "Was my father shot by an Indian?"

"That's what the men said," the medic said over his shoulder without slowing his pace.

Eric turned and faced Still Water. "You shot my father, you…you dirty Indian." He reached to take a swing at her, but Anna caught his arm.

"Don't talk that way, Eric. Still Water did not shoot your father," Anna explained. He struggled to be free, still trying to get to Still Water. "Do you hear me?" Anna asked when she had managed to turn him to face her.

"She did not hurt your father. In fact Still Water was the one who doctored him all the way to the fort," Ingor put in.

The boy was somewhat calmed, but still glared at Still Water. Anna couldn't blame him. All they had heard was that all Indians were bad and should be killed or at least banned from the territory. To meet one that wasn't was a shock, or at least confusing.

"Come on. Let's go see your father, but we'll be quiet in case he's asleep," Anna said to Eric as she took hold of his hand.

Tavis put his arm around Katrin. "Let us know if there is anything we can do," she offered.

Anna nodded and went inside the cabin. She clutched her skirt in her free hand to keep it from shaking. Adam looked so pale against the nearly white pillowslip. The bandages that wrapped around his chest looked new, but already they were soaked with blood.

"Papa," Eric cried, running to climb onto the bed to sit beside his father. "You're not going to die like Grandma and Mama did, are you? You can't die. Then I'll be all alone."

Adam managed to lift his hand and hold his son's. "Don't you worry, son. You will have Anna here to take care of you." Adam looked up to meet her gaze.

"Of course he does," she said. "And right now I think your father needs to rest so he can get his strength back."

"I love you, son," Adam said in a weak voice no more than a whisper before he let go of his son's hand.

"I love you, too, Papa," Eric said as huge tears slid down his cheeks.

Anna held out her arms and the boy jumped down from the bed and went right into them. She lifted him off the floor and hugged him as he wrapped his short legs around her waist. They turned as Katrin and Tavis appeared at the door.

"Eric, why don't you come with us so Anna can stay to care for your father?" Katrin asked.

"It's way past your bedtime, but we can watch them finish putting up the horses," Tavis suggested with a smile. Eric agreed easily and went out of the room with them, swiping his cheeks dry with the back of his hands. "I'll see you later, Father."

Anna walked back to the bed. She was going to pull a chair closer when Adam raised his hand and said, "Sit here close beside me."

She sat on the edge of the bed and offered him a sip of water from the cup on the table by the bed. Once she set the cup down, she took his hand in hers. "Is there anything else you want?" she asked.

"Yes," he said, attempting to smile. "I want you to marry me."

"Ingor is married, but what of the other brother?"

Adam smiled more broadly. "That's part of why I love you so much. You are a woman of honor, and I'm happy to tell you that he is married, too, and already has a child as well."

Tears of joy burned at the back of her eyes and she smiled at him. "In that case, yes, Adam, I will marry you."

"And since I can't seem to move, would you lean down and kiss me, too?"

"I'd be happy to," she said with a grin.

Leaning over, she kissed him lightly, but he raised his head trying to kiss her more firmly. She pressed her lips harder on his, but laid a hand on his head to hold it on the pillow.

"I don't want you to do too much now," she said. "You have a lot of healing to do."

"I am sleepy," he admitted. "And I'm cold."

She pulled the blanket up to cover his bare shoulders. "I'll go see if I can get you some hot broth to drink. And I have to tell the colonel's wife that her plans for a double wedding tonight will have different grooms for the brides. That should be a surprise for the preacher, too."

"Is there a preacher in the fort?"

She nodded. "He arrived yesterday."

"Can you bring him here to see me first?"

"I'll go get him right away."

She leaned over to kiss the back of his hand and by the time she straightened and looked at his face, he appeared to be asleep. Hurrying directly to the colonel's quarters, she found his wife and the preacher sitting out in front. He wore black that was in contrast to his mostly white hair. They rose to greet her when Anna approached.

"How is the lieutenant doing?" the colonel's wife asked.

"Not well, I'm afraid." Anna turned to the preacher. "He asked me to get you. Can you come with me now?"

"Of course, my dear," he said, rising to follow her. When the colonel's wife rose to follow, too, he suggested she remain where she was.

Anna could see the disappointment in her face that she was not allowed to follow them, but she smiled, and with a nod, headed inside her quarters.

"Thank you," Anna said softly. "Adam is terribly weak and his bleeding is worse than ever now. He shouldn't move at all. The wagon ride and getting him undressed and into bed were just too much for him."

"I understand, my child."

They reached the cabin just as Katrin and Tavis returned. "We left Eric with a private assigned to keep a strict eye on him," Tavis told Anna. "We told him he could sleep in his father's bed in the barracks tonight. He feels like one of the soldiers now. If you want him here, all I have to do is whistle for him."

"Thank you," Anna said as they all entered Adam's room.

She thought Adam looked even paler than before. He hadn't moved since she left, but the patch of red on the bandages around his chest was larger. She sat on the edge of the bed and lifted his hand into hers.

"Adam, the preacher is here with Katrin and Tavis, too. They came to see how you are doing."

He blinked his eyes and seemed to have to work to focus on her face. Tavis approached the opposite side of the bed.

"Is there anything you need, sir?" he asked.

Looking at the preacher, Adam asked, "Is that the preacher?"

The man stepped to the foot of the bed and introduced himself. "I would be happy to lead us all in prayer," he said.

"No," Adam said in a voice barely audible. "I want you to marry us—Anna and me, right now."

"Ah, but the colonel's wife has a party planned and…"

"He said right now," Tavis put in firmly. He stared at the preacher until he seemed to digest the urgency of the situation.

"Why of course," he said.

"What about Eric? Do you want him here to see us wed?" Anna asked.

"Yes," Adam managed.

Tavis stepped out the door and with a shrill whistle brought the boy moments later on a run. He swept him up into his arms. "Your Papa wants you at his side. He is going to marry Anna. Can you do that?"

His face brightened by a big grin, Eric nodded. "I'm glad he's marrying Anna, but don't they want to wait for the party?"

"We're going to surprise everyone and get them married now."

Eric ran to stand next to the bed while Anna remained seated by Adam, holding his hand.

The preacher began the ceremony, as they were sure he had done many times before, but Tavis urged him to use a shorter version. The preacher frowned, but went right to asking if Anna would take Adam as her husband. She smiled though her lower lip trembled and said, "I do." He asked Adam if he would take Anna as his wife and he whispered, "Yes."

"Then, I now pronounce you man and wife."

Each breath that Adam took was more difficult. A chilling pain filled his chest. He held Anna's hand and didn't let her go. He didn't want to leave her now that he'd just married her.

Tavis stepped up and picked Eric up. Holding him horizontally, he brought his face near his father's. "Now give your Papa a kiss to congratulate him."

Eric laughed at being held in the air and kissed his cheek. "I'm glad you married Anna, Papa."

"I am, too. I love you, Eric," Adam managed.

Tavis swung the boy up to hold him in one arm. "We'll leave the newlyweds alone now."

He led the preacher and Katrin out of the cabin and closed the door behind him.

That was the last time that Eric saw his father alive. Tavis tucked him into bed in the barracks, and late as it was, he fell right asleep. Katrin was given Tavis' quarters for the night while he slept on a cot near Eric. Ingor and Still Water and the baby slept in their wagon once the bloody blanket had been removed. With only a few hours left to the night, none of them got much sleep.

Anna stayed beside her new husband. She didn't want to break the physical connection for even a moment, so she leaned her head back against his pillow and lifted her legs onto the bed so she lay on her side next to him. Though the only light she had were two candles on the table beyond the bed, she thought the circle of blood beneath him had grown.

She held his hand in both of hers nestled between her breasts, and he opened his eyes to look directly into hers. She forced her trembling lips into a smile. He took a breath and opened his mouth as if to speak, but no sound came out. Only his lips moved and she knew she would never forget his three words that she then repeated softly to him.

Anna's married life was shorter than the night. Adam's grip on her hand weakened soon after the others had left. After a few minutes, his eyes closed and the light went out. His hand suddenly felt heavy in hers, but she held on.

She lay there, holding his cold hand and listening to the silence of the night. Exhausted, she fell asleep. In a brief dream she and Adam danced at their wedding party as the guests all congratulated them. But then the music stopped and the man who had been holding her in his strong arms disappeared. She looked around and saw nothing but rolling waves of tall grass moving in the wind. She felt cold and alone.

Chapter 13

At first light Katrin and Tavis returned to Adam's room. Their soft knock woke Anna. "Come in," she called as she released Adam's hand and rose onto her elbow to return to the sitting position on the edge of the bed. Lifting the sheet over Adam's hand that she had held, she then raised it to cover his head as well.

Tavis extended his arm to help her stand. He held her arm until she was steady on her feet and she and Katrin could leave the room. Tavis went to report to the colonel that the lieutenant had died. Anna went to tell Eric.

The next several days passed in a fog for Anna. She dealt with grieving Eric, showing him the love she had for him. "You will always have a home with me, Eric. You should not ever worry about being alone." He seemed to accept that, and she was glad that she had gotten to know him and Elsie on the journey so that he felt comfortable with her now.

Adam's funeral was held that afternoon and he was buried, with other brave soldiers who had given their lives before him, in the graveyard near the fort.

Following the funeral, Anna and Eric watched as Katrin and Tavis were married in the colonel's living room. Lars and his family had arrived that morning, so both Oleson brothers and their families had attended the funeral and the wedding, too. The newlyweds stayed to join the others for supper, and then went to Tavis' new soddy which the soldiers had finished in the row a half-mile west of the fort.

Anna tried to steel herself for the conversation she should have with the colonel after supper. She and Eric would have to leave the fort now, but she had no idea of where to go. The only place that came to mind was Wahpeton, where the homesteaders said they had hoped that the wagon train had brought them a teacher. She and Eric could never build a soddy, but maybe the neighbors could help.

Or maybe the colonel would have some other ideas.

Before she got a chance to follow him to his office, Lars Oleson asked to speak to her. "We'll be leaving for home in the morning. I… We wondered what plans you have."

Anna held her arms out with her palms up and shook her head slowly. "I don't know what we're going to do." Tears burned in the back of her eyes, but she straightened her back and did her best not to give in to them.

"Everything is happening so fast for you, but we have a suggestion if you would like to hear it."

"Yes, what is it?"

Lissa came from putting their toddler down to sleep in their wagon and stood beside her husband. Lars slipped his arm around her waist. "Let's go outside," she said, "where I can hear if the baby cries."

"Let me ask Rose to keep an eye on Eric, and I'll be there in a moment," Anna told them.

A couple of minutes later they stood in the middle of the open area in the fort where they could hear the baby, but their talking would not wake him.

Anna clutched her hands together at her waist over her stomach that was churning. She smiled at the Olesons and was about to ask them what they had in mind when Ingor and Still Water joined them. Their baby was fast asleep in the carrier on her back.

"We want to be a part of this, too," Ingor said.

"You have just arrived and already the tragedy must have made your life here seem impossible," Lissa said.

Anna nodded and tried to force her trembling lips into a smile. "Yes. I feel lost and now I have Eric to care for, too. I just don't know what I will do." Tears stung in her eyes, but she took a deep breath and refused to give in to them.

"We have been talking, and since we are responsible for bringing you here, we would like to suggest something that you can do," Ingor told her.

"It could be a good life for you and Eric," Lars added.

"And we would certainly like it," Lissa put in with a smile.

"Please. Tell me what it is," Anna said.

"All right," Lars began. "We got the idea for you because three months ago the wife of the man who was homesteading about a mile from us…well, she died giving birth to their first child." He held up his hand to stop any comment from Anna. "After she died he didn't want to stay there. He wanted to go back to Ohio where he had family who could help with the baby. It was a shame, because he had built a unique soddy, and they were happy there."

"A soddy?" Anna asked.

Lissa nodded. "Yes, the closest one to ours."

"I don't know how to live in one, but I guess I could learn," she said tentatively.

"You'll like this one. It's a good-sized house with a bedroom separate from the living room and kitchen area that are together. Then he went on to build a smaller bedroom for the baby off the back, where the warmth of the fireplace would reach it to keep it warm. On the other side of the living area, he built an extension, like we have, for a horse or two and cow so they would be protected during storms. He took the horse when he left, but another neighbor is caring for his cow. It would be yours."

"But how could we live in someone else's soddy?" Anna asked.

"He left," Lars put in. "He abandoned his homestead. He told everyone that he would not be back, and we'd like it if you…you and Eric, would come to live there."

"But I am no farmer," Anna protested. "I wouldn't know what to do to be a homesteader, and Eric is too young to even ride a horse alone. He needs to be cared for and wouldn't be any help."

"We know that, but you don't have to farm the land. We can help you register your claim. We can mail the application before we leave the fort. And all your neighbors would help you plant trees, too."

"Trees?"

"That's all that has to be done to improve the land is to plant trees."

"I don't have to farm the land?"

Lars shook his head. "You can plant trees instead."

"After you live there a certain number of years, the land will be yours," Ingor explained.

"But how could we succeed? I have little money and couldn't buy even food to last us very long, much less trees. We wouldn't last a year."

"We think you could," Lissa insisted, laying her hand on Anna's arm. "Eric has told us about all the books in his grandmother's trunk. We brought some out west with us, too."

Anna shook her head slowly. "I cannot make soup from books."

Lissa laughed. "No, but Katrin told us that you would have been a teacher if you had stayed in Norway." Anna nodded. "We want you to open a school."

"A school? But where?"

"At the homestead," Lissa replied.

"The living room of the house is big enough for several children to sit at a long table. Wally could build the table for you, and the chairs, too. We have enough wood for that," Lars promised.

"We lined our wagon floor with planks when we came west and we'd be happy to have him use some for you," Lissa offered.

"I don't know what to say," Anna admitted. "You make the impossible seem so possible." She took a deep breath.

"There are other families with several children within a few miles of that homestead, and they all would love to have a school to send their children to," Lars said.

"They could pay you in food from their gardens, or chickens, or whatever you needed," Lissa said.

"We could all help plant your trees, too," Ingor told her.

"There's already a garden by the house that you can grow food in, too," Lissa added. "Once we get the weeds out, it should do fine."

"A garden would be good, but I'm a woman. Can I have a homestead in my name?"

"Yes, you can. You are the head of a household now, Anna," Lars reminded her.

"I can hardly believe what you are telling me." Tears welled in Anna's eyes as she truly began to understand that her future could be bright. "I…I didn't know what we would do and this sounds wonderful. How can I thank you?"

"Does this mean you think you would like teaching?" Lissa asked.

"I would love it," Anna replied, smiling despite her trembling lower lip.

"It will help that you speak Norwegian and English. There are a lot of Norwegian families in the area. You can help the children learn English, and they can help their parents," Lars added with a laugh.

"And the homestead? The land truly will be mine to pass on to Eric?"

"You won't have any trouble proving up with all of us to help."

"Proving up?" Anna asked, not knowing the phrase.

"That's what the government calls following all their directions until the land is turned over to you. Even with no husband, it will be your land in your own name."

"This is perfect. Now I can't wait to tell Eric in the morning."

"Anna, it won't be easy. You'll have to work hard like we all do, but you'll have many people to help. And more are coming west each year," Lissa told her. "They're starting a settlement over on the James River, and it won't take long before we have a town near us."

"So much is happening, and I must tell Eric."

"If you can't find him he may be with my brother," Lissa said with a smile. "He wants to learn how to whittle the little wooden toys that Wally is always working on, too."

"Oh, dear, isn't he too young to handle a knife?" Anna asked.

"Well, you don't have to worry about that now. We can keep him busy getting the place ready for you to live in. It has been empty for a few months."

"We'll make sure the soddy is sound with a good roof and chimney. It was well built so it should be in good condition," Lars put in.

"I will have to learn how to live in a soddy, but this chance to be a teacher for the children is wonderful. I can't thank you enough. Oh, I must tell Katrin. She will be so surprised."

"Ah, I know this is sudden and I hate to rush you, but we're leaving in the morning. We can't be away any longer. There's too much to do at home."

Anna frowned. "We'd be happy to take you there with us," Lars told her, making her frown disappear. "There's room on our wagon for

Elsie's trunk and any other cases you have. The colonel said his men packed up Adam's personal things so you can take them, too."

"Yes. Eric will want them someday," Anna said.

"I will enjoy the company in the wagon," Lissa said. "Will you come?"

"Yes, I will come with you." Anna wiped at the errant tears that made it down her cheeks as she turned to Ingor and Still Water. "I worry about you and the baby. Are you going back to where the Indians attacked Adam?"

Ingor nodded. "Yes, it's our home. Still Water is certain that it was a small band of Indians that came into the Dakota Territory to raid for food and supplies before they went back to Canada."

"But Ingor shot the leader of the band, so it's not likely that they'll be back," Still Water added.

"But I have to ask one more question. I need to know this about the homestead that was abandoned: are there Indian raids there?"

"Hasn't been one since we moved there," Lars replied easily. "With more soldiers here, the government is getting ready to make a big push to get them all to move out of the way of so many white folks coming in."

Anna smiled and looked from one of her new friends to the next. "I think this is a wonderful thing you all do for me and Eric, and I will be your teacher. We will work together. I have to learn to be a teacher in America, just as I have to learn to be a mother to Eric."

"We know you will be good at both jobs," Lissa assured her.

"I can leave with you tomorrow morning, but I must tell Katrin all about it. She and Tavis have already gone to their new home. I hate to bother them now when they are just married." She laughed away her embarrassment at mentioning it.

"We can stop there on the way by in the morning," Lars assured her.

"Good, then we go. I think Eric will be quite excited. The colonel said we should take Adam's horse," Anna told him. "You will have to tell me how to care for a horse and for a cow."

"Finding a small cart for the two of you to ride in won't be impossible," Lars added. "His horse should be able to settle into riding in a harness."

"We still have the wheels from my father's delivery wagon. Wally might like the challenge of making a small two wheeled cart for you," Lissa told her.

"So much to think about. I won't sleep a wink tonight," Anna said with a little laugh.

They set a time for their departure right after breaking their fast in the morning. Lars and Lissa were certain the colonel would give them paper to write to the Homestead Office about taking over the abandoned homestead. They bid Anna good night and she went to find Eric. They had talked so long that Sergeant Stanton was now keeping an eye on him as he slept in his father's cot again in the barracks, so she had no worries there. She would tell him in the morning.

Anna wished the sergeant a good night and returned to the room she had shared for a few hours with her husband. Moving by the light of a small fire someone had built in the fireplace, she lit the candle on the table. She saw that the bloody mattress and linens had been removed and replaced with clean ones. She moved to stand in the warmth of the fire.

The Olesons had erased the dark future that she thought would be hers. The opportunity to be a teacher would give her life meaning and the method to provide for Eric. It would be a good life for her, and for Eric, her son she loved dearly.

She would always regret losing Adam, the man she had come to love. A day wouldn't pass that she didn't think about him, but dwelling on the life they might have had together would get her nowhere. The new opportunities open to her now were quite amazing, and she was willing to work hard to make them a reality.

She removed her dress and washed up. Without bothering with her nightgown, she slipped into the bed in her shift. She pulled the blanket around her shoulders and gave herself only a few moments to wish Adam's arm were around her before she fell asleep.

* * * *

"We're going to live in a soddy?" The grin on Eric's face could not have been broader and he could not have been more excited about going with Lars Oleson's family to a homestead of their very own. "That means we'll live nearby Wally." He had become friends with Lissa's brother, and they had talked of all the things they could do together.

"Anna will be counting on you being a big help, Eric," Lissa told him as they loaded the wagon the next morning.

"What can I help with? I can't even ride a horse."

"Well, one of the first jobs would be weeding the vegetable garden to save the vegetables that the previous homesteader had growing there."

Eric made a face and shook his head. "I don't like vegetables very much," he said, losing some of his enthusiasm.

"You like soup and stew, don't you?"

"Sure. I like them but not vegetables." He turned to run to Anna and Lars who came from writing the letter to the Homestead Office.

Lissa laughed as she watched him run. She thought she'd wait to let him learn that soup and stew were packed with vegetables.

"Get home safely, will you?" Anna said to Ingor and Still Water, whose wagon was ready to leave. "And thank you for all you did for

Adam. I don't think he would have lived long enough to marry me without your help."

"He saved my life by stepping in front of me to protect me," Ingor told her. "I will always be thankful to him. He was a good man."

"A good man? I agree, but you didn't know him," Anna said.

Ingor smiled. "No, but when he saw Still Water with a rifle in her hands, he didn't shoot her."

"He ordered his men not to shoot either," Still Water added.

Anna nodded her understanding.

"I wish I could have done more for him," Still Water told her.

"You brought him to me alive. Thank you," Anna said. "I wish you well and I hope you will come visit us."

"We'll be there with trees to plant as soon as we can. There are many young shoots in the woods behind our cabin. There's time to get them in the ground before hot weather, but you and Eric will have to water them over the hot summer." Ingor helped his wife and son onto the driver's bench of their wagon. "He'll like playing with pails of water," he added with a laugh as he mounted his horse. Everyone waved as they rode out the open gate and headed north to their cabin.

"That's everything," Lars called as he put the boards across the back of the wagon to keep the contents from falling out. He tied the Indian mounts that Ingor had left for Anna on the back before he lifted Berg and Eric into the wagon. He put Anna's small bag under the seat next and lifted her and Lissa up to the driver's seat.

"Here's another thing I have to learn. I have never driven a team of horses pulling a wagon," Anna said once she was settled using her larger bag as a cushion. She was crushing her wedding dress again, but this time it didn't matter. She'd never gotten to wear it and could only imagine using the fabric as curtains on a window, if there was one, or maybe just covering the wall like she'd seen in the Wahpeton settlement.

"Don't worry. You'll know how to drive a team by the time we get to your homestead," Lissa promised with a laugh.

While Lars and Wally rode their horses, Lissa turned the wagon and drove out the gate. They all turned west toward the soddies where the soldiers with families lived.

Katrin heard the wagon coming and came out with Tavis, who was ready to go report for duty at the fort. He stayed with her as Anna explained where she was going and what she and Eric were going to do.

Anna thought the newlyweds looked so happy being together. She was happy for them.

"I'm so surprised, but I can see that you are feeling good about it," Katrin said. She turned to Lissa and Lars. "Thank you for thinking of it. Tavis and I talked about what she might do, but we didn't come up with any plan as good as this one."

"I will miss being near you, Katrin," Anna admitted. "We have been through so much together."

"It won't be impossible to visit her," Tavis assured Katrin.

"And maybe we'll have a homestead near yours when Tavis leaves the Army," Katrin told her. "That will be next spring. Wouldn't that be wonderful? Then we could see each other as often as we wanted."

The sisters hugged tearfully as they parted. "Be happy, Anna," Katrin said softly. "Adam would want you to be."

"I think we will be," Anna admitted with a shaky smile. "It won't be easy, but I'm determined to succeed for Adam, so his son can have a good life."

"I think he would be proud of what you are doing," Katrin told her.

Anna couldn't speak past the lump in her throat. She hugged her sister again and let Tavis kiss her cheek in a farewell gesture. As she waited for Lars to give her a hand up into the driver's seat, she wiped the tears that had streaked her cheeks.

"Goodbye," Eric called with an energetic wave as they pulled away.

Traveling to the homestead in the Oleson's wagon was very different from crossing Minnesota in the hired coach. However, Anna hoped it wouldn't rain, because there was no way to protect anyone or anything in the open wagon. She looked up to see the bright blue sky spread from horizon to horizon. Didn't look like rain would fall any time soon.

The Dakota Territory they rode through was very different from Minnesota, too. Anna hadn't really believed it when she'd heard it, but there really were nowhere near as many trees here. Many of the ones they did see had grown bent by the wind that seemed to blow most of the time across the prairie. They didn't pass lakes either.

Once, in the distance to the north, Lars pointed out slews that were crusted in white all around. "They're no good for man or beast," Lars said, staying on track to go past them.

They stopped to spend the night beside a stream suitable for drinking. The women and children slept in the wagon while the men slept under it. Lissa, Wally, and Lars each slept with a rifle next to them.

Anna was reminded that she didn't even know how to load or shoot a rifle either. That was another necessity for survival that she had to learn. It suddenly occurred to her that she did own one, however. She had seen Lars wrap Adam's rifle and side arm in a blanket with boxes of ammunition and pack it in the wagon. She would have to thank him for thinking of it for her. She never had.

They reached the abandoned homestead the second afternoon. The grass had grown high in front of the soddy and it was covering whatever was growing within the fenced garden beyond. Between the garden and the soddy, Anna saw two poles about chest-high rising out of the grass. A cross piece from one pole top to the other had rope wound around it and a pail hanging beneath it.

"Is that the well?" Anna asked.

"Yes." Lars walked over to it and lowered the pail. They all heard it splash and walked over to see it when he wound it upwards full of water. "You have water," he said, cupping his hands and lifting water from the pail to show her.

"The sides of the top of the well are sod blocks and they're not very high. Eric, you will have to stay clear of the well. Oh, dear. With other children here for school, I would always worry about them getting too close to the well and falling in."

"You're right, but we can fix that," Lissa told her. "Lars can cut more blocks and they can build the sides higher and thicker."

"That would be much better," Anna said.

"But don't forget that all the children come from homes that have open wells like yours. They know to stay away," Lissa replied.

"I had forgotten," Anna told her as they all walked toward the soddy.

Lars pulled out clumps of grass growing along the front door and opened it. He stepped inside. With a startled squeak, a mouse ran outside nearly running over his feet. Anna watched it disappear into the tall grass.

"We'll clean those out for you, but you have to be sure to plug any holes in the sod walls or they'll move in for the winter."

"Oh, dear," Anna murmured. She'd never had a mouse problem where she lived in Norway.

She and the others followed Lars into the soddy. Looking around the room in the light from the open front door, because there was no window, she saw that only the larger pieces of furniture like the one wide bed were there, though any straw mattress that might have been on it was gone. A worn table only a meter wide was left near the fireplace, but there was only one chair, and it was lying on its side.

Wally picked up the chair and looked at the legs. "The top is broken off one leg, but I can shorten the others a bit to match it, and Eric, you can have a lower chair to sit on."

"I can sit on a big chair," Eric insisted.

"All right then," Wally countered. "Then Anna will have her first chair for one of her smaller students."

"I guess I could sit on it for now," Eric allowed.

"And I guess you'll have to sit on the bed until you get more furniture," Lissa said to Anna with a smile for Eric.

"I can make you some more chairs," Wally told her. "I'll get to work on the long table for your students, too."

"Oh, look on the wall," Anna said with her first smile. "He left the shelves on both sides of the fireplace."

Lars walked over to them and tugged on them. "They seem sturdy. The supports go a good way into the sod blocks."

"We can get an early start on the work in here," Lissa announced. "But let's get a fire going now for light before we lose the sunlight."

"Eric, come on. I'll show you how to knot the long dry grass so you can use it to start a fire," Wally said. The two of them walked out of the soddy.

Turning back to the door to watch them go, Anna looked behind the open door for the first time. "Oh, look." She walked toward a large galvanized washtub that hung from a peg driven into the wall like the shelf supports. "How wonderful. I was wondering if I'd ever be able to take a bath again," she said with a relieved laugh.

"The homesteader couldn't fit it in his wagon," Lissa guessed.

"I'll carry it outside. You can learn how to use the well and put some water in it to be sure it doesn't leak," Lars offered.

While the women followed his suggestion, Lars checked the walls and then climbed onto the roof while he had the daylight. "There's one area that's soft, but the rest all looks good. It will last a good long time."

"Look what Wally got," Eric called.

Eric pointed his arm toward Wally who carried two dead rabbits, one in each hand that he held up high.

"He caught them in the garden," Eric said proudly." He showed me how, but I missed getting one."

"But you learn quick," Wally said. Eric grinned. "There are a lot of them out there so you'd better get them before they eat all your food. I can show you how to set a snare tomorrow."

"You two go clean them, and I'll get a fire going in the fireplace," Lissa said.

Outside, Wally showed Eric how to clean rabbits. "I'll show you how to treat the rabbit skins so you could use them. They're good size," Wally said. "There will be enough fur for a hat or mittens for next winter." They gave the meat to Lissa who showed Anna how to cook the rabbits on the cast iron spit that the homesteader had left over the fire.

The boys stayed outside sitting in the grass where Wally began to scrape the inside of the fur clean with his knife. As usual, Eric was watching his every move.

"Do you think Anna knows how to sew fur?" Eric asked, trying to clean the second skin.

Wally shrugged. "I don't know, but your mother is smart. She'll figure it out."

Eric looked at him with a frown. "My mother? She died when I was born."

"I mean Anna. She's your mother now, isn't she?"

"I don't know. I've never had a mother, only a grandmother." Eric looked up at him. "Do you have a mother?"

"I did," Wally replied. "She was sick, and died while we were coming west."

"Like my grandmother did."

They worked in silence for a few minutes.

"Would you like to have a mother now?" Wally asked Eric.

"Jimmy liked having a mother. They rode in our coach with us. I think I'd like it, too."

"Then you might ask Anna if you can call her mother. She might like it, too."

Eric looked at Wally and then at the soddy where Anna had stepped out to call everyone to supper.

Chapter 14

Lars rode off from Anna and Eric's homestead the next morning, but he was back traveling at a slower rate before noon. Tied to his saddle was a milk cow that was balking at having to keep walking. He had balanced a basket of eggs packed in grass so they wouldn't break, a loaf of bread, and a slab of smoked bacon on his pommel. He handed the foodstuffs to Anna. "These are from the Hansen's, your neighbor to the north," he told her as he got off his horse. "They also sent half a sack of oats." He untied it from behind his saddle. "I'll put these in the soddy until we clear the mice out of the barn. No sense feeding them these good oats."

"I told the neighbors all about you and Eric, and they are very happy to have a school beginning near them. They have four children. Besides that, I got the good news that there has been no Indian trouble since we left for the fort."

"And the cow? Is that the one the homesteader left?" Anna asked.

Lars nodded. "I'll drive a stake into the grassy area in front of the soddy where you can tie him. You just have to move the stake when he's eaten the grass there. Eric, you can help Anna by checking during the day to be sure the rope doesn't twist around her legs. Of course, she needs to be milked each morning and evening. She'll let you know if you forget."

"I forgot about milking her," Anna said. "I know how, but I have no milking pail."

"You do now," Lars said, untying a pail that hung from the pommel on the other side of the horse's neck. "Comes with the cow," he added with a laugh. "They're going to bring a few chickens when they come.

I couldn't figure out how to carry them."

"There is so much to think of to figure out how to provide for Eric and myself. I'm used to going down the street to a store when I need something."

"You've got a good start here and if you have to, there's nothing wrong with cooking the oats a while to soften them good. They're not bad to eat when you have nothing else."

"Stop, Lars, you're scaring her," Lissa told him. "You're not to worry. When the word gets around that you have moved in, the parents of any children around here will come to meet you, and I promise you that they all will bring you food. They all know what it was like to start out here."

Anna and Lissa soon cooked a little of the bacon with eggs. They captured every drop of bacon fat and running egg yolks with the bread.

"We'll make frames from twigs from that bush growing by the soddy after supper," Wally told Eric as they ate. "Then we stretch the hides over them to cure. When that's done, you take the fur off the frames and work to soften it."

"I think everything out here is work," Eric told him.

"You're pretty smart to figure that out so fast." He patted Eric on the back.

They had eaten outside the soddy, sitting in the grass again. Having a bit of milk to drink was a treat. They chose to sleep out there as well. Having the fire in the fireplace helped move fresh air through the soddy, but it needed another day to smell fresher. Anna and Lissa had gotten the floor swept clean and then spread on water to give it a hard surface. It dried over night so in the morning the men moved the trunk and cases inside.

Lars climbed up on the roof then, too, and added clumps of sod where he thought it might leak. "We won't know if this is good until it rains, but the boards under the sod are still good. I can patch it again if it leaks."

"Ours leaks a little when it's a real gully washer," Lissa said. "But it's fine in most rains, and the grass growing up there helps dry the blocks out fast."

While clearing the garden area, Wally and Lars cut the grass from the roots and piled the grass in the washtub. When they were done, they carried the tub closer to the soddy and spread the cut grass out on the grass growing there. "This will dry quickly and then you can use it to fill mattresses," he told Anna.

"I'm glad we brought fabric. I didn't like having to carry all the weight, but I can use it to make the mattress cases."

"I'll bet Ingor can come up with some furs to keep your beds warm by this winter," Lissa said. "We all use the ones he gave us."

"Along with the rabbit furs," Anna said with a laugh.

They discovered that the original owner had gotten some wheat and oats planted that spring in a small area beyond the garden.

"That must be all he had time to clear," Lars said. "We'll come help harvest it at the end of the summer. Having more oats then will ensure the horse will have something to eat when the deep snow has buried the grass."

"It won't be much wheat, but it would give you enough grain to grind into flour for bread or flapjacks for you and Eric," Lissa guessed.

"Ingor said he'd bring a few trees soon, but most of the planting to improve the land will begin the next spring," Lars told Anna. "You'll have your hands full just unpacking, settling in, and getting the soddy ready for your students."

There was one more matter that Lars made sure was done before dark. He took Adam's rifle and side arm out of the wagon and showed Anna how to load it and shoot it. He made her practice over and over, until he was convinced she would remember how. It hurt her shoulder when it fired, but she was glad he had taken the time to explain it all.

"You may have noticed the pegs in the wall over the door," Lars said. "They are for setting the loaded rifle there where you can reach it easily if you need it, but it's high enough to be out of reach for Eric and the other children."

"And like the open well, I think the other children will be used to seeing a rifle there," Anna replied.

Lars nodded. "Children grow up fast out here. They learn early on what can be dangerous and they stay clear of it. They know there's no help nearby if they get into trouble."

"Yes, what happens here can be a matter of life or death. That is the hard lesson that Eric and I have already learned."

* * * *

Saying goodbye the next morning was not easy for either Anna or Eric though he brightened when Wally promised he would be back as soon as he finished the long table and chairs. The Olesons left the straw that had been in the wagon to pad the ride for the boys.

"Now we have straw and grass for the mattresses," Anna said with her thank you's.

Anna and Eric waved as they rode off to their own homestead. They watched until the wagon and men on horseback disappeared from view.

Anna looked down to see that Eric was staring after them and he didn't look happy.

"How would you like to go on a treasure hunt?" she asked.

His face bloomed with a big smile. "Yes, I think that would be fun."

"Come on. I know just where to hunt."

He followed her into the soddy and over to Elsie's trunk. "I think this is the perfect place to hunt. Let's see what we can find."

She opened the trunk, and they began to remove the treasures.

"I'd like the books lined up on the shelf beyond the fireplace. Let's see if they fit," Anna suggested.

Eric couldn't reach the shelf, so Anna lined up the books, laying a few down at each end to hold them there.

"Why don't you pick one that I can read to you in the evening? Would you like that?"

"Yes." He pointed one out right away. "Grandmother started to read this to me, but she never finished. I'd like to hear the end."

"This one it is," Anna said, taking out the book and handing it to Eric. "Why don't you put it on the corner of the bed frame."

Eric set it there and they both went back to the trunk.

"So many things." Anna said. "What shall we take out next?"

She continued to involve Eric in the unpacking in a fun way as the day progressed. They removed dishes, cups, bowls, and pots and pans, and set them on the table. Anna lifted the dish set up to the shelf on the wall that was on the opposite side of the fireplace from the bookshelf. She had to set the bowls and pots and pans on the end of the stone hearth.

Over the next several days, they continued their treasure hunt. Elsie had packed much more utilitarian fabric than Anna had brought. Thankful she didn't have to use fabric that might be made into a dress for her some day, or a shirt for Eric, she used Elsie's fabric to make them each a mattress. Eric helped fill them with the straw and grasses that had dried in the warm sun. There was only one bed frame in the room that went back beside the fireplace, and Eric insisted that Anna put her mattress on it. He wanted to sleep on the floor in the main area.

"You don't want the small room they built on the other side of the fireplace?"

"Maybe when we've lived here longer. It smells like wet mud now."

"You can sleep where you want. Sleeping here will be cooler this summer and this winter you can move closer to the fire," she said.

He grinned. "By winter Wally promised he would make me a bed frame."

"How good of you to strike that bargain. And what are you going to do for him in trade?"

Eric frowned. "I'm too little to do anything."

"Well, Eric. You can be a friend to him and to all the children who come to our school."

He grinned broadly. "That would be easy."

"Good."

With only the daylight and the small cooking fire she kept going to see by, she turned a dress of Elsie's that was way too small for her into a tablecloth for the small table, where they would eat their meals when inside. She would put it on to cover the cuts and worn spots when they weren't using the table. Others might think it foolish, but Anna thought having the bit of cheer of the flowered fabric was good.

When the trunk was empty of things they could use in the soddy, Anna had Eric put his extra clothing in one side and she put hers in the other.

"This will work until something better comes along, and the trunk will keep the mice out. That's good, because I don't think the clothes will fit them."

Eric laughed at her joke.

The neighbors began to visit to introduce themselves and to meet Anna and Eric. Lissa had been correct. Each family brought gifts of food. Anna learned from each of them and their experiences surviving on the plains. Two families came together and built a small chicken coop in the yard for them. They added four chickens and told Anna how to care for them.

"When winter comes to stay, you can kill one at a time and enjoy chicken for dinner, because they won't make it outside in the freezing weather," one man told her.

"She's got the barn. She might get a few to stay in there for the winter. Them ponies and the cow will put off the heat," the other suggested.

"You could sure try it," he allowed.

Lissa's brother soon returned with the long table for the students to use and wooden boxes that he had made for their kitchen. "Lissa stands boxes like these on end along the wall and keeps her kitchen things in them."

"What a good idea," Anna told him.

Eric helped him put them in place and immediately went to the hearth to get the bowls and pots and pans. They all fit with room to spare.

Eric was very excited that Wally had also brought several chairs made like milking stools with three legs and no back.

"I also brought longer legs for the chair you have with the back. I'll put them on so you can have a chair at a comfortable height, Anna. These stools will be fine for the children during class. While the weather is nice, I think you'll be outside and sitting in the grass where the light is better," Wally said.

"And one of the stools will be perfect for sitting on when I milk the cow. I've been doing that kneeling on the ground."

"Glad it will work," Wally said. He didn't stay long and made the return trip home the same day.

Eric helped when Anna cut odd pieces of cloth from the bodices to stuff into good size square pockets for hot pads. She needed them to hold the cooking pots and to move them aside when she put more wood on the fire.

The remainder of the summer was just as busy. Many neighbors who had been so helpful visited them again. They all agreed on the date that school would start. One family had a brother coming from Pennsylvania in the spring. They wrote to him asking that he bring slates and chalk for all the students.

Though the slates wouldn't be there for most of the school year, the students arrived bright and early on the appointed day. Anna watched as they chose a seat at the long table that she and Eric pushed against the wall when school wasn't in session. Not much learning happened that first day, but then Anna and Eric learned all the children's names. She smiled watching him play games with them outside.

Under the royal blue sky with the sun to warm them, they stayed outside after playtime for a lesson in how to write their name. They smoothed the dirt with their hands and wrote with a round pointed stick that Wally had whittled for each one.

Anna surveyed the group of children bent over their task with a smile. Everything and everyone around her here in the Dakota Territory was so different from back in Norway, but she liked them all. Her life here in her new home was certainly different from the one she expected—the one she hoped for. She had lost the man she loved, but was blessed with his son to love and care for. Now she was blessed with several more children to teach.

After the children left that afternoon, Eric came to her and took her hand in his. "Come on," he said. "I want to show you something." He led her to where the children had been writing their names. "I wrote your name, too, after they left for home."

She looked down expecting to see Anna written in the dry earth. That isn't what she saw. There was only the word "Mother."

"May I call you mother?" Eric asked in a small voice.

Tears burned in her eyes as she knelt beside him. "I would be very happy to have you call me mother," she told him.

He threw his arms around her and hugged her. A moment later, he was heading for their soddy. "Come on, Mother," he urged. "Isn't it time to fix supper? I'm hungry."

Yes, life was different than she ever expected, but life was good.

About the Author

Lois Carroll, who also writes under the name Lois Schwartz, has been writing since her childhood, when she received a daily diary as a gift. With a bachelor's degree in English Literature and a master's degree in Theater, she began her writing and editing career as a copy editor at a publishing company. Now a wife, mother, and grandmother, she writes full time. She lives with her husband in the desert of southern Arizona. When she's not writing, she's working on her service project, Sophie's Smocks, that has given away hundreds of feeding/craft smocks free to kids and adults with Angelman Syndrome. To date she has published five hard cover books, eight paperbacks, over a dozen e-books, plus short stories and non-fiction articles in national magazines and journals. You can read about her available books and email her through her web site at

: http://loiscarrollbooks.com/

31585496R00127

Made in the USA
San Bernardino, CA
15 March 2016